"Why don't we stop playing games? Let's quit acting like there isn't a mutual attraction sizzling between us."

"There is no attraction," Naomi threw back at him caustically.

"Don't deny it. The chemistry has been there from the moment we met."

"Only a rich, arrogant millionaire intent on getting his greedy hands all over my company would say that." She rose from the chair she was seated in. "Neither I nor my company is for sale, Lucius."

She stalked out of the lounge with as much dignity as she could muster given that he was partly right. There was something there between them. She had to be on her guard with Lucius at all times. She couldn't—wouldn't—fall prey to his charms like most of the women he encountered.

She was in the elevator and the doors had nearly shut when Lucius caught up to her and worked them open with his large hands before stepping inside.

They were alone in the elevator.

He walked purposely toward her, and Naomi automatically shrank back a couple of steps. But when she did, her back hit the wall—not a good position to be in with a dangerously sexy man like Lucius.

Dear Reader,

I came up with the Knights of Los Angeles series after watching the television show *Empire*. I loved the name Lucius and the family dynamic of brother against brother, and thus the idea for *Taming Her Tycoon* was born.

This book focuses on corporate raider Lucius Knight's quest to learn his parentage. When he does, it will rock his world. All the while, Lucius has his eye on former tomboy turned businesswoman Naomi Brooks. He wants the lady and her organic-products company, but can he convince her that mixing business and pleasure would be oh-so-satisfying? The series will conclude with his brother Maximus Knight's fight to retain his empire.

My next book, *Miami After Hours*, will be available June 2017. In the meantime, feel free to visit my website at www.yahrahstjohn.com or write me at yahrah@yahrahstjohn.com for more info.

Best wishes,

Yahrah St. John

Taming Her Tycoon

YAHRAH ST. JOHN

HARLEQUIN® KIMANI™ ROMANCE

Recycling programs
for this product may
not exist in your area.

ISBN-13: 978-0-373-86481-2

Taming Her Tycoon

Copyright © 2016 by Yahrah Yisrael

HARLEQUIN®

Printed in U.S.A.

™ www.Harlequin.com

Yahrah St. John is the author of twenty-two books, fifteen of which are under Harlequin Kimani Romance. Yahrah hails from the windy city of Chicago, where she earned a bachelor of arts degree in English from Northwestern University. She currently resides in the beautiful city of sunny Orlando. Yahrah was nominated for an RT Reviewers' Choice Award in 2011 for *Two to Tango* and was the winner of an RT Reviewers' Choice Award in 2013 for *A Chance with You*.

St. John is a member of Romance Writers of America, but is an avid reader of all genres. She enjoys Broadway shows and concerts, reading, cooking, traveling and watching professional basketball, and she is an adventure sport enthusiast. But her true passion remains writing. For more information, please visit www.yahrahstjohn.com.

Books by Yahrah St. John

Harlequin Kimani Romance

Two to Tango
Need You Now
Lost Without You
Formula for Passion
Delicious Destiny
A Chance with You
Heat Wave of Desire
Cappuccino Kisses
Taming Her Tycoon

Visit the Author Profile page at
Harlequin.com for more titles.

Chapter 1

"**I** want Brooks and Johnson," Lucius Knight told his lawyer and best friend, Adam Powell, as the two sparred in the boxing ring of their favorite gym on a Wednesday afternoon. It was one of Lucius's favorite pastimes when he needed to blow off some steam, and today was one of those days.

"I know. I've been acquiring the shares like you asked, but why?" Adam inquired as he squared off against his six-foot-two friend.

Lucius put his gloves down and looked him in the eye. "Does it matter? I want it."

"Yeah, it does," Adam said. "I've never seen you so focused on a company before. Why is it so important to you?"

Lucius couldn't tell Adam the real reason he was interested in Brooks and Johnson, an organic retail company, was its cofounder Naomi Brooks. Known for his playboy lifestyle, Lucius hadn't been able to settle for anyone or anything, let alone a woman. But Naomi Brooks was different. He liked her story. She was a no-nonsense type of woman, a real do-gooder who not only believed in what she was selling—organic products that ranged from shampoos and conditioners to body lotion—but had also become successful in her own right. Who would have thought that the nerdy sophomore with the boyish figure and acne problems who followed him around during his senior year in high school would someday turn her basement business into a national success story?

Lucius understood that kind of determination.

Because he'd done the same thing. A reformed bad boy turned businessman, Lucius had experienced a chaotic relationship with his mother and had chosen to live with his grandmother in the Rose Park neighborhood of Long Beach.

Adjusting to the neighborhood and being a loner hadn't been easy for Lucius. He'd rebelled and gotten into trouble often in school. Eventually, he'd met Adam, and a friendship that would last decades had been formed. Lucius had gone on to obtain an MBA before investing in his first business venture, an up-and-coming technology firm. The gamble paid off, and he'd made his first million before he was thirty. And thanks to his shrewd sense for recognizing opportunities, he'd formed Knight International and was now a wealthy tycoon with holdings across multiple industries.

"Hey, hey." Adam waved a gloved hand in front of Lucius, jolting him from looking back down memory lane.

"You do that again and you'll get knocked out," Lucius joked, effectively ending their conversation about Brooks and Johnson.

"I doubt that." Adam gave him a jab in the side. "Who do you think taught you how to fight?"

Lucius answered with a blow of his own to Adam's middle. "You did. But as in the stories of old, sometimes the student becomes the teacher."

Adam laughed heartily. "We'll see about that."

The two men continued to spar for another hour before they finally took a break. The gym along Santa Fe Avenue was starting to fill up with locals, which signaled it was time for Lucius to roll. Even though he still liked coming to the old neighborhood because it reminded him of days gone past, Lucius also knew the hundred he'd paid to the kid outside to watch his Bentley to ensure no one would scratch it wouldn't last too much longer.

"How about a beer?" Adam said as they jumped down from the ring and walked toward the benches where their gym bags were.

Lucius smiled as he reached for a towel to wipe the perspiration from his forehead. "After a shower, you're on."

"Kelsey, whatever you're cooking up smells wonderful," Naomi Brooks said from her bar stool as she watched her business partner and best friend, Kelsey Johnson, stir a fragrant concoction on the stove of her four-bedroom home in Belmont Shore that afternoon.

Kelsey shrugged her shoulders, tossing her blond curls. "It just kind of came to me. I've been stirring this pot for an hour trying to get the consistency just right."

"In your condition—" Naomi eyed Kelsey's growing belly "—you don't need the extra exertion. Plus, we have a development team that handles new creations for us."

Kelsey turned from the stove to face Naomi. "I'm only six months pregnant, not completely fragile. And I kind of miss the days when it was just the two of us toiling away on our new business."

Naomi nodded. She remembered those days, too. How could she forget? She and Kelsey had had the bright idea of starting an organic-products business eight years ago due to the sensitive skin and allergies they had in common. Naomi had suffered terribly in high school with bad acne. It had just been a notion, but soon they were in the kitchen testing out their ideas. Their parents had thought they were crazy. They'd just received their four-year liberal arts degrees and now their daughters wanted to start a new business with no experience?

They'd shown them.

Naomi and Kelsey had researched the hell out of the organic industry and slowly started building their brand. They initially sold candles, shower gels and bubble baths from Kelsey's apartment. Word of mouth about their little business began to spread in the local community, especially when they began attending farmer's markets. Soon, they were expanding to include shampoos and conditioners. And once their business hit a stride, they could no longer make their products out of Kelsey's apartment. There had been some serious discussion about the next steps for their growing business. They'd also decided that selling online rather than going retail was the best way to promote and market their products.

It worked.

Their online presence had quadrupled their sales, causing the need for an office and a manufacturer who could distribute their growing product line. Once they'd topped several hundred million in revenue, they'd moved forward with an IPO and gone public, putting 49 percent of their shares on the open market but retaining 51 percent. It was important that they maintained majority interest in *their* company.

Naomi glanced at Kelsey. It was hard to believe just how far they'd come. "It was just the two of us for a long time," she finally commented wistfully. But times had changed. Especially when Kelsey had two miscarriages and had a difficult pregnancy with her first child, Bella. Since then,

Kelsey had opted to work from home, only coming into the office when needed.

"I know." Kelsey stirred the concoction in the pot. "But having this second baby is making me reevaluate things and think about what's more important."

Naomi frowned. She didn't like where this conversation was going. "What do you mean?"

Kelsey sighed heavily. "I'm thinking about whether I want to stay in the business."

Naomi jumped off her bar stool and walked over to Kelsey at the stove. "Why? I don't understand? Where is this coming from? Is Owen putting pressure on you to quit?"

Kelsey stepped away. "He would rather I focus on our growing family and he has encouraged me to sell. He thinks the stress of pregnancy and working full-time has taken a toll on my body. And he's right, to a degree, but I'm torn. Brooks and Johnson means a lot to me, but..." Her voice trailed off.

"But what?"

"I don't know. It's just not the same anymore like when we first started out. Some of the joy has gone out of it."

"Because we're successful?" Naomi inquired. "It's what we've always wanted, what we worked so hard for." She turned away and walked over to the sink and grabbed both sides with her hands. "Or at least I thought so."

Several seconds later, she felt Kelsey's hands on her shoulders. "Don't be mad, okay? I'm just being honest and telling you how I feel. Just like I did when I first met you and saw you needed a little help in the beauty department."

Naomi chuckled and turned around to stare at Kelsey. At five foot four, Kelsey's petite figure was still recognizable even though she was expecting, due to a regime of vegan food, yoga and Pilates. "Don't sugarcoat it now. I believe you called me a hot mess."

Both women laughed.

"Well, you were," Kelsey responded with a grin. "You had acne and you wore your hair in a ponytail, and the clothes…" She snorted. "You were straight out of the '90s. You wore those baggy jeans and plaid shirts. It was no wonder you couldn't get a date."

Naomi rolled her eyes.

"Now look at you." Kelsey eyed Naomi's figure up and down. "Your skin is clear and bright from using the proper facial products. And you finally listened to me telling you relaxers were killing your good hair, so it looks healthy now."

Naomi fingered the soft spiral curls that reached her shoulders and complemented her long face. She'd fought Kelsey in the beginning about going natural, but the look suited her. Though it had taken some practice and a good stylist to learn how to work her natural curls into coil and twist styles, she'd mastered it. "Yeah well, I'll give you that one."

"And?" Kelsey countered. "Look at your clothes? We finally found your style—bohemian chic."

Naomi was wearing a bat-wing sweater with distressed jeans, fringed boots and clunky jewelry adorning her ears, neck and wrists. She was finally learning to show off her killer size-four figure. "I can't thank you enough," Naomi replied, "for taking in such a socially inept, fashionless woman as myself, but that still doesn't change the fact that you're ready to bail on our business after all we've endured."

Kelsey stirred the mixture on the stove one more time before turning off the burner. She was quiet for several long moments before responding. "You know I love you,

Naomi, but my priorities have changed. I have to put my family first. But listen, I'll give this some more thought before making any decisions."

Naomi gave her a bear hug. "Thank you. That's all I could ask. But while you're figuring things out I'll be doing the same. Perhaps I can buy your shares."

"Naomi, that would be a steep sum and a lot of responsibility. Can you afford it and are you really ready to take on all the responsibility?"

"I don't know, but I have to find out," Naomi replied. Because although Kelsey posed some good questions to give Naomi pause, she had to *do* something. Otherwise, the future of Brooks and Johnson, a company they both started, was in jeopardy.

After showering at the gym, Lucius and Adam headed to a local gentlemen's club they liked to frequent. The service was top-notch and the scantily clad women that delivered them their drinks more than made up for the overpriced menu.

"Ah." Lucius sipped on his scotch neat and leaned back in the lounge chair to face Adam. "I needed this after that workout."

"Yeah." Adam nodded. "Seems like you had some steam to let off today. What gives?"

Lucius shrugged. "It's nothing." He wasn't altogether keen on talking about the real reason for his bad mood.

His mother, Jocelyn Turner.

"Bull," Adam stated. "I know when you have something on your mind."

Lucius frowned at Adam. He could always read Lucius even though outsiders never could. Lucius strove to always have a poker face in his business dealings. Most people never knew what was going on in his mind, and he liked it that way. It kept people off-kilter and gave him the element of surprise, which he needed when deciding whether to take over or dismantle a company.

But Adam knew him too well.

"It's Jocelyn," he replied. "She's coming to town." His grandmother Ruby had told him his jet-setting socialite mother would be stopping in for one of her semiannual trips.

"Oh." Adam nodded his head thoughtfully. "That explains it. How long is she staying?"

"Don't know. Don't care."

Why should he? Jocelyn Turner had never cared about him. He'd had countless nannies before she'd finally sent him to a junior boarding school at the age of nine, and he'd acted out accordingly, so she'd handed him over to his grandmother. And bless her heart, his grandma done right by him. She'd brought Lucius to live with her in Long Beach and tried to instill good values in him, but Lucius had always known he was an afterthought.

His mother didn't want him, and his father? Hell, he didn't even know who he was, and Jocelyn refused to tell him no matter how many times he asked or pleaded. Lucius had begun to suspect that his father was a married man. So what did that make his mother?

At a young age, he'd learned to harden his heart and toughen up. It was a lesson that had served him well in life and in business. Of course, it also happened to get him in a lot of trouble as a teenager. His grandmother had been called constantly because he was getting in fights or being suspended from school. Lucius had gotten something of a reputation in high school as a bad boy because he rebelled against authority. Meeting Adam had changed his life and shown him he wasn't as alone as he'd felt in the world.

"I don't think that's true," Adam interrupted Lucius's

musings. "It's because you care. Every time your mother visits, you get riled up."

Lucius took a long drink of his scotch. "That's not true."

"Do you remember the last time she was here? You were so out of sorts that it nearly cost us that Corinth deal because you insulted the man right when he'd agreed to not fight you on the takeover."

"Yeah, well, he deserved it," Lucius commented, even though he knew Adam was right. His hotheadedness was one of his flaws. "Speaking of takeovers, let's talk about Brooks and Johnson."

"Ah, are you ready to tell me why you're so interested in the company?"

"Have you seen the numbers they've been bringing in?" Lucius commented. "They've grown steadily over the last three years, and their revenue is impressive and can double now that they've been public for a few months. And I've learned that one of the principals might be open to selling. So we should strike while the iron is hot."

"Kelsey Johnson or Naomi Brooks?" Adam inquired. "Why would either of them sell?"

Lucius rubbed his chin. "Didn't the dossier on Kelsey Johnson say she's pregnant with child number two? She could be thinking of downsizing and focusing on her family. That could be our in."

Adam leaned back in his chair. "I would think business is the last thing on her mind."

"We need to convince her that now is the right time to sell."

"And what about Brooks?"

"Let me handle her," Lucius said. He was eager to reconnect with his high school classmate and see how the once nerdy kid he remembered had turned the tables and become a successful entrepreneur. He'd also seen a picture of her recently, and she'd blossomed into a fine-looking woman. A woman he wouldn't mind getting to know better.

"You should be aware that Lucius Knight has been silently buying up Brooks and Johnson's stock since the IPO," Bill Andrews, Naomi's vice president, told her the next morning after they went over some company business.

Naomi was leaving for Anaheim later that afternoon because she wanted to get a jump on traffic leaving Long Beach. She would check in to the hotel, pick up her registration packet and get settled before the trade show and conference started tomorrow. But first, she'd come into the office to take care of a few items. She hadn't expected Bill to tell her that corporate raider Lucius Knight, her former high school crush, was interested in her company.

"Since when?" Naomi asked, staring up from her MacBook.

"A couple of months ago," Bill responded. "At first I dismissed it, but then Knight International recently picked up another 5 percent, making his total stake in the company 30 percent."

Naomi closed her MacBook. "That's not good."

"No, it isn't," Bill said. "Every time Lucius Knight sets his sights on a company, he either dismantles them or they wind up as part of his portfolio."

"But why would he be interested in us?" Naomi asked. "We're a far cry from his other holdings." She too had done her research on the man. Ever since college, she'd kept her eye on her former crush—Knight International had a mix of industries in its portfolio, but they were mainly centered on technology.

Bill shrugged. "He could be looking to diversify. And given the success of Brooks and Johnson, he could get in on the ground floor. I received a call from his attorney Adam Powell—he'd like a meeting with you."

"A meeting?" Naomi hated that her voice hitched and the question came out more like a squeak.

"How would you like to handle it?"

"Ignore it," Naomi responded. "I'm not interested in talking to Lucius about my company or anything else."

Bill stared at her.

"What?" she snapped. She knew Lucius was a large shareholder, but she didn't care. "Why are you looking at me like that?"

"Because I haven't seen you this passionate before unless perhaps we're talking about a new product or launch."

"Well…well, I just don't like the thought of Knight thinking he can railroad me or my company. I'm no one's pushover."

"Never thought you were, Naomi," Bill replied. "What you and Kelsey were able to accomplish is phenomenal."

Naomi's burst of anger fizzled, and she smiled back at Bill. "I'm sorry if I was a little abrupt," she said. "I just get angry at the thought of someone trying to take something I worked so hard to build."

"We won't let that happen, Naomi. But he's a major shareholder now."

"I'm aware, Bill." She began packing her computer and some work files into her leather briefcase. When she was done, she snapped it shut and reached for her purse inside a drawer. "However, I trust that you'll keep the hounds at bay at least while I'm at the conference. When I get back, we'll address this." She started toward the door.

"Absolutely, boss."

"I'll see you when I get back." Seconds later she was headed toward the elevator lobby.

She stabbed at the down button as she waited for the elevator.

Lucius Knight wanted her company? Her baby? Hell, no. There was no way she was going to let the man—no matter how good-looking—weasel his way in and take over everything she'd built. She would show him and every other local who'd discounted her in high school and thought she was less than just how strong she'd truly become.

Chapter 2

"Grandma." Lucius softened his tone when he heard his grandmother's voice on the other end of his iPhone. "It's so good to hear from you."

"I hope that remains the case when you hear what I have to say," she replied.

"I could never be angry with you, Grandma." He loved the older woman with all his heart. She'd been the only mother he'd ever known and the only person who loved him unconditionally, except maybe Adam. "What's going on?"

"I spoke with your mother today."

"And?"

"Don't act dense, Lucius. It doesn't suit you," she responded. "She said you haven't returned her calls."

"I know."

"Well, when do you intend to?"

Lucius snorted. He hated the reproachful tone in her voice. He counted from one to three to remind himself to remain respectful. Grandma Ruby deserved it. She hadn't had to take him in when he was a young boy. She'd raised all her children. Three, to be exact—his mother, Jocelyn, his aunt, Deborah, and his uncle, Troy. But she had taken him in. And she'd been in his corner ever since.

He finally responded. "Soon."

"I wish you two would try to get along," his grandmother said. "It takes so much energy to hold on to all the bad blood."

"Have you told her this?" Lucius asked. "The only thing I've ever asked of that woman is tell me who my father is. And to this day, even though I'm thirty-four, nearly thirty-five years old, she refuses to tell me."

"Perhaps some things are best left unsaid."

Lucius was silent. He'd always wondered if his grandmother knew the truth, but she'd point-blank told him that if she did, she would tell him.

When he continued to remain silent, his grandmother said, "I have to go. I'm heading to the grocery store, but do go and see your mother, Lucius. You might regret one day that you never resolved things between you. Promise me you will."

He was being guilt-tripped and he didn't like it. "All right, Grandma. For you, I'll make the effort. Satisfied?"

"Immensely. Love you, Lucius."

"Love you, too, Grandma." Lucius ended the call and sat back against the plush cushions of the limousine. He knew she meant well, but her meddling in his and Jocelyn's relationship wouldn't help the situation. He would never see eye to eye with his mother until she was honest with him about who he was.

Until then, they'd always be at an impasse.

Naomi was excited as she checked in to the Anaheim Hilton. A valet immediately greeted her when she disembarked from her car and took care of her baggage while she checked in to the hotel.

She glanced around and took in the modern decor done in beiges and dark wood. It was classic yet modern. It would serve as a good backdrop for the natural products expo where she hoped to get Brooks and Johnson even more into the public consciousness. She wanted people to start using their products, which were now inclusive of not only personal care products, but home cleaning products and a new baby line as well.

The baby line was Kelsey's brainchild. It was still in its early stages but included baby washes and baby powders. They would soon expand to include diapers, rash cream and wipes. Naomi was just as passionate about having organic products for her goddaughter, Bella, and her soon-to-arrive godson, Caden.

With Lucius Knight circling like a vulture, Naomi just hoped that she could convince Kelsey not to sell her shares so they retained majority interest in the company they'd built.

"Good afternoon, Ms. Brooks," the front desk attendant greeted her. "Great to have you back with us again."

Naomi smiled. "Thank you. I'm glad to be back."

"I can't tell you enough how much I love the Brooks and Johnson body wash and lotion line. It's done wonders for my skin." The attendant caressed her cheek.

Naomi beamed with pride. This was exactly what she liked to hear when meeting customers. "Glad to hear it!"

"We've put you in one of our signature suites, complete with a queen-size bed." She handed Naomi two room key cards. "I sincerely hope you enjoy your stay, and if there's anything else you need, please don't hesitate to let me know."

"Thank you, and I will." Naomi accepted the envelope and headed for the elevator bank.

* * *

Just as Naomi entered the elevator, Lucius's limousine pulled up to the Hilton's entrance. Just as he'd promised his grandma Ruby, he'd called Jocelyn. Thankfully she hadn't answered, so he'd left a message, giving him a reprieve from an unpleasant conversation.

The chauffeur opened the door of the limo, and Lucius stepped out, buttoning up his suit jacket as he entered the building. He was used to five-star establishments but knew that he needed to get in front of Naomi Brooks. He'd heard that she would be attending the expo, and the only way he could do that was to be as approachable as possible. Thus, he would stay in the same hotel with all the other attendees and exhibitors.

Content to handle business himself, he made short order of checking in. After obtaining his card, he headed for the elevator.

Some might consider his tactics a bit sneaky, but he needed to figure out Naomi Brooks. What were her strengths, her weaknesses? A smart businessman knew his opponent, because only then could he use the knowledge to his advantage. He was determined to add Brooks and Johnson to his portfolio. Having a company of that caliber under his wing would only lend itself to making Knight International more credible. He didn't just want to be known as a corporate raider. He also wanted to be known as a man who stood for something, and this acquisition would give him credibility.

Disembarking from the elevator, Lucius headed to his two-bedroom suite. He glanced down the hall, wondering where Naomi was staying. It was just a matter of time before they met.

Naomi dressed simply yet professionally for the trade show and conference the next day. She'd knotted her wild curls into a bun off her face to show off her neck and cheekbones. Then she teamed a crisp three quarter sleeved white shirt with a taupe pencil skirt and a thick brown belt with matching heeled sandals. She finished the look with a gold bangle set and long gold necklace. She glanced at herself in the mirror. The outfit was suitable for the office and could transition for an evening afterward.

She grabbed her briefcase and hobo purse and excitedly hurried toward the door. Fifteen minutes later, she'd already checked in with Brooks and Johnson's event coordinator to make sure their booth was being set up and would be ready when the trade show opened later that afternoon. Assured that everything was under control, Naomi decided she could attend some of the workshops. Perhaps they might give her some inspiration?

She found one to her liking and headed to the right convention room. They were just starting, and there were many empty seats in the back of the room, so Naomi slid into one of them.

She was listening rapturously to the professor when she felt the seat beside her suddenly become occupied.

The scent of cedar washed over her nose as a strong thigh brushed against hers. Naomi's breath hitched in her throat as she tried to focus on the lecture and not on the man sitting beside her. Whoever this stranger was, he smelled delicious, and Naomi couldn't resist licking her lips.

"Good topic?" the deeply masculine voice asked from beside her.

Naomi didn't turn around. She didn't want to. For just a little bit longer she wanted to stay enveloped in his scent and let her imagination roam as she wondered who the owner of the rich masculine voice and sensual cologne was.

"Yes, it's very timely," she commented.

"Undoubtedly."

Naomi frowned. The masculine voice beside her sounded familiar. Like she'd heard it dozens of times before, like when he'd told some bullies in high school to leave her alone. Except now the voice had matured and was stronger, more confident. Naomi turned and stared directly into the dark brown eyes of Lucius Knight.

Does she recognize me? Lucius wondered. *Or does she just know of me? Is she aware I'm after her company?*

Naomi didn't speak for several seconds; she just eyed him warily before turning back to face the front of the room. He could feel her tense beside him almost immediately. He'd hoped their first meeting would be smoother. He prided himself on his ability to charm the socks off almost anyone, including most women, but it seemed Naomi wasn't interested.

Instead of replying to his earlier comment, she continued to focus on the lecture until the hour was complete. When it was over, Naomi rose and so did Lucius. "So where are you headed?"

She glanced over her shoulder at him. "To gather info and maybe learn something like everyone else." And without another word, she left his side and walked up the aisle to speak with the professor. Lucius had no choice but to take action.

He purposely walked toward the duo. "Professor Duvall, great talk," Lucius said.

"Coming from you, Mr. Knight," the professor said, "that's quite a compliment."

Naomi said nothing from his side. Lucius could see she was fuming, because he hadn't taken the hint to take a hike. "Lucius Knight." He turned to her and offered his hand.

She would have to shake it if she didn't want to appear

unprofessional. When she did, Lucius was surprised by the reaction he felt when their hands touched. There was a spark, but she also didn't offer her name. Instead, she snatched back her hand.

"I'm eager to hear more, professor. Perhaps we can have coffee sometime later?" Lucius reached inside his suit jacket and produced his business card. "Call me." He nodded to the professor and strode purposely toward the door. He'd accomplished what he'd intended. Naomi knew he wouldn't be ignored.

Lucius stepped away to take an emergency call from Adam about another acquisition and missed the next few lectures and a chance to catch up with Naomi.

After he'd put out the fire and grabbed some lunch, he was ready for the trade show that opened at 3:00 p.m. He showed his badge and was allowed entry into the show. He was perusing many of the exhibit booths that ranged from agriculture and beauty to fitness products when a certain curly-haired updo caught his attention.

Naomi.

Lucius made a beeline in her direction.

She was bent down, smelling some cocoa beans, when he approached.

"Smell something you like?"

You, Naomi thought when Lucius's familiar scent drifted toward her. He probably tasted just as sweet as one of the organic milk chocolates in front of her. Why did she have to run into him now? She wasn't ready and hadn't had enough time to put on all her armor. Nor was she in any way prepared for the depth of the attraction she'd felt at the merest touch of his hand earlier.

It had startled her. That now, nearly sixteen years later,

Lucius Knight would still have an effect on her. She was no young ingenue anymore.

"Did you hear me?"

Naomi blinked several times, bringing Lucius back into focus. "Excuse me?"

"I asked if you smelled something you like." He inclined his head to the cache of cocoa beans she was holding.

"Oh, yes, it has some interesting notes that might work well for one of my product lines."

"You own your own business?"

Naomi rolled her eyes. Really? Were they really going to play this game? Well, if he wanted to act like he didn't know who she was, she would do the same. "Yes, I do. I own a line of organic personal and home care products, among other things."

"So this expo is right up your alley."

"Yes, and you? Why are you here?" Naomi realized her question was blunt, but it was to the point.

Lucius smiled but answered. "I own a variety of businesses and am interested in expanding my reach. The rise of organic products and healthy living has really caused me to evaluate what I want to venture into next."

"Sounds reasonable." Naomi handed the beans back to the exhibitor and began moving to the next table.

Much to her chagrin, Lucius followed. "How long have you been in business?"

"Eight years."

"Impressive. Not many start-up businesses make it past the first year."

Naomi shrugged. "We had a lot of support from the community. And you? How did you get your start?"

Lucius stared at her sideways. He seemed surprised by the question but answered her anyway. "I had a knack for determining companies worth investing in."

"How vague," Naomi replied.

An amused smile crossed his face as he looked down at her. And Naomi swallowed, shifting uncomfortably in her sandals.

A strange invisible pull was between them, and Naomi didn't like it. Nor did she like the way Lucius stared at her like he wanted to gobble her up with a spoon or something. What was happening between them? It didn't make any sense. She hadn't seen him since she was fifteen years old, when he'd graduated from high school. She shouldn't be feeling this way. Not again. And not now. Not when Lucius wanted to take away something very precious to her.

"I have to go." She walked to another table several feet away.

"Why?" Lucius asked to her retreating back. "I thought we were finally getting somewhere."

"Oh, yeah? Where was that?"

"If we're both lucky, to a bedroom."

His arrogant and shameless words caused Naomi to turn on her heel to face him. "What did you just say?"

Lucius's smile was devastatingly handsome and also a bit devilish as he walked toward her. "You heard me. But if you want to act like you didn't feel what I felt when we touched earlier or just now, I'll bite and play the game."

"Of all the nerve." Naomi refused to even give what he said credence—even though he was right. If the simplest of touches could cause that kind of reaction, it was obvious there was something underlying, but Naomi wouldn't be acknowledging it. Instead, she turned and walked away.

"Naomi, Naomi." She heard her name being called and could see Alexis, her intern, waving her over to the Brooks and Johnson table. When she'd hired the interns, she'd told them that they were all on a first-name basis and could call her Naomi.

"No need to yell, Alexis," Naomi said when she arrived. Her salespeople were already occupied with other customers, so Naomi headed straight for her. "What can I do for you?"

"Well, this gentleman wants to know how they might go about carrying our products at his stores," Alexis replied with a smile.

Naomi smiled and hid her purse under the table. Now *this man* she could handle and knew what to do with. She immediately started explaining Brooks and Johnson's mission statement and how they would be a great addition to his business. It didn't take long for the man to hand her his card and tell her he'd be in touch to talk terms.

"That went wonderfully," Naomi said five minutes later to Alexis, who was standing avidly by, soaking it all in.

"How'd you do that?" the young woman asked. They'd hired her to help with the trade show and she was still green.

"Experience," Naomi replied. "Don't worry, the more you're exposed to these types of environments, the more you'll learn."

Applause sounded from behind Naomi. She didn't need to know who was praising her. Lucius. The man refused to go away. He was like a puppy nipping at her heels.

"I couldn't have said it better myself, Naomi Brooks," Lucius responded. He held out his hand. "Pleasure to officially meet you."

Chapter 3

Naomi thought about leaving Lucius hanging, but since she was in front of her intern, who looked to her as a mentor, Naomi had no choice but to accept the handshake. Lucius's hand clasped her small one, and a ripple of excitement went up her spine at touching him again. He studied her face, waiting for a reaction.

Damn him!

She quickly released his hand and turned to her intern. "Alexis, I'd like you to meet—"

"Lucius Knight?" the girl finished. "*Black Enterprise* businessman of the year."

"One and the same." Lucius smiled broadly, and Naomi couldn't fail to notice he had straight, pearly-white teeth. His charm hit the poor intern like a ton of bricks, and she blushed from ear to ear, her cheeks turning red.

"Oh, my God!" Alexis's hand flew to her mouth. "It's a pleasure to meet you."

"You as well," Lucius said and turned back to stare at Naomi. His eyes pierced hers, and Naomi felt her heart hammer foolishly in her chest. She hated that she was having such a reaction to his obvious interest in her. If this had been sixteen years ago when she'd loved his rebel-without-a-cause image, she would have welcomed it, but not today.

"You could learn a lot from this woman," she caught Lucius saying. "Naomi and her partner started this company from nothing and have grown into a multi billion-dollar enterprise, or so I've heard, while I've just gambled on the right companies."

"Clearly your gambles paid off," Naomi responded.

Lucius laughed heartily. And Naomi had to admit she liked the sound of it. "They usually do."

"Arrogant," Naomi muttered underneath her breath.

"What was that?" Lucius asked.

"Oh, nothing," Naomi said. "Alexis, I'm going to get back to the trade show. The salespeople are available—" she motioned to her sales team, who'd finished with their customers "—as am I if you need me again, all right?"

"Sure thing, Naomi." Alexis smiled.

Naomi retrieved her purse and started toward the other table, but stopped. "Are you coming?" she asked Lucius. Since it was obvious she wasn't going to shake him, she might as well try to use his interest to find out more about what he had in store for Brooks and Johnson.

His face creased into a sudden smile. "Love to."

Lucius was happy that Naomi softened toward him as the afternoon progressed. If she'd kept the hardened stance from earlier this morning, he would have his work cut out for him. But this more laid-back Naomi was more his speed. And if he played his cards right, their relationship would be more than just business.

When he'd seen her sitting there in the workshop, he couldn't believe his luck. It was an opening for him to get to know Naomi and how she'd changed from awkward teenager to brilliant businesswoman. He hadn't found out everything he wanted to know about Brooks and Johnson that afternoon, but he enjoyed her company. Perhaps it was because he found Naomi extremely attractive.

A luscious mane of spiral curls was piled atop her head, allowing him full view of her delicate neck and shoulders. Or was it the way she carried herself now? She was more confident and assured in that pencil skirt that hugged all the right places. The white shirt, though professional, gave him just a hint of cleavage that he was dying to find out what secrets were underneath.

Lucius didn't know this version of Naomi Brooks. He remembered a gangly teenager who was so socially awkward the students in their high school made fun of her. He'd protected her once when a gang of bullies razzed her. Adam probably thought he didn't remember, but he had. She'd looked so small and innocent back then, unable to take care of herself.

But this new Naomi Brooks was a force to be reckoned with. Lucius had a feeling that a takeover of her company wouldn't be as easy as he'd thought. Naomi wasn't just going to lie down and roll over. She was going to fight him, but Lucius was more than ready for the challenge.

"How about a cocktail?" Lucius asked when they'd both seen enough of the east wing of the trade show and everyone was starting to pack up for the end of the day.

"I don't think so."

"C'mon," Lucius said. "What are you going to do? Go back to you room and order room service?"

Naomi chuckled, and Lucius suspected that was exactly what she was going to do. "Only if I get to take off this outfit and put on something more comfortable."

Visions of Naomi naked sprang to Lucius's mind, but he blinked them back. "Deal. How about I meet you downstairs in the lounge in fifteen minutes?"

"You're on."

* * *

Ten minutes later, Naomi paced her hotel room after she'd changed into jeans and a tank top and let down her hair. It was her usual attire after a long day, but the reason why wasn't. Why had she agreed to a drink with Lucius? The man couldn't be trusted. He'd already acted like he didn't know who she was when she knew darn well he'd done his research on her. Did he remember they'd gone to high school together? Did he remember when she'd followed him like a lovesick puppy dog after he'd saved her from some bullies?

Of course he didn't. He was Lucius Knight, international playboy and heart stealer. Why would he remember a gangly, pimple-faced teenage girl?

It was no wonder her heart had palpitated around him, because that was Lucius's appeal. He reeled women in then tossed them aside when he was done. She'd read the tabloids, seen him with gaggles of beautiful women, models and actresses alike. Naomi wouldn't become one of those women.

But those dark eyes. They seemed to look into her soul. And those lips…they were full and kissable.

Stop. Stop. Stop.

She had to remind herself that she was in control. Of her own destiny and her company's fate. She would and could resist Lucius, even if he turned on his full charm, which she was sure he would do tonight. But she would be on her guard.

Lucius rose from his lounge chair when he saw Naomi enter the room. Damn, the woman was fine as hell! She made ripped jeans and a tank look like she was wearing the slinkiest dress ever. As she walked toward him, Lucius was aware of how the jeans rode low and snug around her hips. How the tank clung to her breasts, tapering down to her narrow waist. Lord almighty, he was in trouble.

"Naomi." He pulled out her chair.

"Lucius." She sat down and he joined her in the opposite chair.

"What can I get you to drink?" He motioned the nearby waiter over.

"I'll have a pomegranate martini."

He rattled off her order to the waiter and turned back to face her. "I like you in casual attire. It suits you."

"More than my business attire?"

Lucius shook his head. "Not more than, just that you appear more yourself."

"And how would you know that?" she countered.

He dodged her question. "Am I wrong?"

She laughed and leaned back in her chair. "No, I prefer jeans to suits and skirts, but it's a necessary evil at times."

"Agreed. So tell me, Naomi, how does someone as young and vibrant as you decide to take on starting her own business?"

Naomi shrugged. "It might have been a notion to some, but Kelsey and I—that's my business partner," she added, even though he already knew this information, "didn't want a nine-to-five job. We wanted to be in charge of our own destiny."

"I can understand that," Lucius responded. "I wanted the same thing. To be my own man."

"From the looks of it you succeeded," Naomi replied.

"Wow. That sounds like an insult coming from you."

Naomi shook her head. "Not an insult, just the truth. You've done quite well for yourself, Lucius Knight. Not only are you in the business magazines as a self-made millionaire, but you're also in every gossip rag, thanks to your dalliances with beautiful women. Unlike most rich men, you're not spoiled, but you definitely have their confidence and arrogance."

"And I take it those are traits you don't admire?"

"Quite the contrary. I admire confidence and believing in oneself."

"But not my arrogance?"

Her brow rose. "Wasn't it you who pretty much *ordered* me to meet you down here for a cocktail?"

"I didn't order you. You were welcome to decline the invitation."

"I doubt you would have taken no for an answer."

He threw back his head and let out a peal of laughter. She was right. He wouldn't have taken no for answer, not when he suspected that Naomi found him equally as attractive as he found her. "All right, Naomi. I suppose you're right. Would it also surprise you to know that I knew who you were before we met?"

"Not at all. My vice president informed me of Knight International's interest in *my* company."

The waiter returned with their order and placed the drinks in front of them.

He noted her emphasis on the word *my*. Naomi knew of his desire to control Brooks and Johnson, which made her a formidable adversary. "So you've prejudged me? You should know my interest is not only professional, but personal."

Naomi chuckled, reached for her drink and took a few calming sips before answering. "C'mon, the only reason you're trying to charm me is so you can find out more information on Brooks and Johnson."

"That's not the only reason." Lucius sat upright and leaned closer to her. His eyes caught and held hers over the circle of light from the votive candle on the table between them. His dark eyes bored into hers and spoke without words of his desire for her. She dropped her eyes under his intense scrutiny.

Naomi might be confident in business, but just then he'd seen a flash of the old Naomi. The sensitive, innocent Naomi who'd once admired him. Now, however, he didn't want her admiration—he wanted her to *want him*.

Naomi couldn't hold Lucius's gaze and lowered her lashes. His eyes had darkened dangerously with what Naomi felt was akin to lust. His face was hard and lean, just like his body. A body that was emphasized by the wine-colored polo shirt that revealed his bulging biceps and black jeans that showed off his trim waist and long legs.

Naomi felt an unwelcome surge of excitement. Her body felt heavy and warm due to his unrelenting gaze. She reached for her drink, and Lucius caught her hand. Naomi's pulse pounded at the smoldering flame in his eyes.

"Why don't we stop playing games? Let's quit acting like there isn't a mutual attraction sizzling between us."

"There is no attraction," Naomi threw back at him caustically.

"Don't deny it. The chemistry has been there from the moment we reconnected."

"Only a rich, arrogant millionaire intent on getting his greedy hands all over my company would say that." She rose from the chair she was seated in. "Neither I nor my company is for sale, Lucius."

She stalked out of the lounge with as much dignity as she could muster given that he was partly right. There was something there between them. She had to be on her guard with Lucius at all times. She couldn't—wouldn't—fall prey to his charms like most of the women he encountered.

She was in the elevator and the doors had nearly shut

when Lucius caught up to her and worked them open with his large hands before stepping inside.

They were alone in the elevator.

Lucius glanced at the elevator buttons. "We're on the same floor, fate is bringing us together."

Then he walked purposely toward her, and Naomi automatically shrank back a couple of steps. But when she did, her back hit the wall—not a good position to be with a dangerously sexy man like Lucius. His hands splayed on either side of her face, caging her in.

"You do want me," Lucius countered, "even if you won't admit it." He reached for a strand of her hair and twirled it around his index finger. "How about we put your resolve to the test, hmm?"

Naomi caught the challenging gleam in his eye right before his lips descended on hers. Naomi thought the kiss would be hard, but it was soft, as were his lips. She'd always wondered what they'd taste like, and now she knew. He sipped at her lips until she gasped and a low moan escaped her lungs. Lucius used it to his advantage, demanding full entry between her lips at the same time his hands slipped from the wall to cup her bottom so he could press her to him.

Naomi felt his hard, flat stomach and his broad chest as he held her firmly to him. She also felt the swell of his erection that sprang to life against her stomach. His hands ran up and down her body, and Naomi trembled.

Lucius lifted his head long enough to stroke her hair back from where some had fallen around her face, his eyes searching hers for a sign to stop. Finding none, he lowered his mouth once more to engage hers. He kissed her top lip, wetting and nibbling it with his tongue before going to her bottom lip. He sucked on it voraciously, and Naomi felt her nipples become taut and expectant. Of what?

Of Lucius's mouth on them?

The elevator doors suddenly opened, and Naomi sprang from his embrace as if they were two randy teenagers caught making out underneath the bleachers. The bellman smiled at them both and pressed the button for the next floor.

Clearly, he knew what they'd been up to.

Did she?

What had possessed her to kiss Lucius back? Naomi knew what Lucius wanted, and she had no intention of succumbing. And as soon as the bellman was gone, she would tell him so.

She didn't have to. Once he'd disembarked two floors up, Lucius turned to her. "That was bad timing. I should have waited until we were in my room."

"Your room?" Naomi asked. Her shoulders squared. "I'm not going anywhere with you."

Lucius's hand rubbed his neatly cropped head. "Really? Are you going to act like you didn't enjoy that kiss just now? Like if that bellman hadn't interrupted us, you wouldn't have been mine for the taking?"

"Of all the…" Naomi stabbed at the elevator button. She couldn't wait for her floor to arrive.

Lucius leaned back against the wood paneling inside the elevator, regarding her quizzically. He watched the rise and fall of her chest, and his gaze immediately dropped from her eyes to her breasts. Was he assessing their size? Did he prefer huge breasts to her B-cup ones?

His eyes returned back to her face, and she felt flushed. He couldn't know what she was thinking, could he?

"All right, Naomi. I'm going to let you go tonight."

"*Let* me go?"

He smiled at the challenging tone in her voice. "That's right. Because, trust me, if I tried, I could seduce you into my bed tonight, but I won't. I want you to come there willingly."

"There is no way in hell that's happening."

The elevator chimed and doors opened, indicating it was their floor. She stepped out and turned around long enough to hear Lucius say, "We'll see. We'll see."

Chapter 4

Naomi was in a foul mood the next morning for the final day of the conference. She hadn't slept well, having tossed and turned due to the melodramatic threat Lucius made the previous evening. He'd made it clear that the inevitability of them becoming lovers was a foregone conclusion.

Was he right?

Naomi didn't want him to be.

Or did she?

He was right in that they had chemistry in spades, but how could there not be when he stared at her like he was dying of thirst in the desert and she was his oasis? It was enough to put any red-blooded woman on alert.

Once she'd returned to her hotel room, her mind had gone haywire. The memory of Lucius kissing her, his tongue delving deep inside her mouth, the way her nipples had turned rock hard along with the telltale sign of wetness between her legs, tormented her. It had been shocking how turned on she was by one kiss from Lucius. Naomi's face flamed at the realization she'd wanted him—or at least her body did.

Was this a sign that her former crush on Lucius had

never gone away and instead had just been buried deep in the recesses of her mind until his kiss brought it forward?

Why did this have to happen now? When she might possibly have to fight to keep her company? If Kelsey did indeed want to dissolve their partnership and sell her shares, it would leave Naomi vulnerable to an attack from Knight International. And not just on the business front. Lucius was coming for her *personally*.

She'd seen the determined look in his eye last night as the elevators doors shut. A look that told Naomi he meant to have her.

Would she be strong enough to fight him off when her own traitorous body found him irresistible?

Lucius woke up the next morning feeling surprisingly refreshed given there was no valet or butler to assist him for the day. He was on his own. And perhaps that was just as well. He suspected that to get through to Naomi he would have to be himself.

There were no airs to Miss Brooks. Instead, she was a woman who appreciated the simple, basic things in life. So he was sure it came as a shock to her that she too could be led astray by the desires of the flesh. She'd probably been bedding nice guys who had no idea how to bring out the vivacious woman he'd seen last night.

But she was there. He'd seen it in her eyes and body language.

And he was just the man to bring out the sensual side of her nature. Once he got her alone, he would seduce her. Last night, when his hands had roamed over her body, he'd had just a sample of what it would be like to touch that beautiful body of hers, and he craved more.

An added bonus was that while he was rattling Naomi's cage, Adam would be working on Kelsey. The soon-to-be second-time mother might be his way to get enough shares of Brooks and Johnson for a takeover.

But first things first—he had a certain woman to woo.

Downstairs in the convention center, Lucius discovered that finding Naomi wasn't all that easy. If he didn't know any better, he'd think she was avoiding him. After reading the itinerary for the second day of the expo, he attended a lecture he'd thought would surely interest her, but when he'd arrived he'd found the lady wasn't in attendance. Nor was she in the second lecture later that morning.

Lucius was quickly becoming annoyed that he'd yet to spot her—until he arrived at the trade show. Naomi was standing in front of her display talking to several customers. And she was doing a heck of a job. She'd convinced him, and he was only standing a few feet away.

She looked feminine in a sleeveless pink wraparound top and gray slacks and pink peep-toe pumps. Glittering silver earrings adorned her ears and only emphasized her beautiful face, on which she wore very little makeup other than a touch of blush, mascara and pink lipstick.

When she was done and had handed her business card to one of the customers, he applauded her.

She turned, and when she saw him, her smile faded. "Lucius."

"Good morning," he responded, not allowing her lackluster response to faze him. "I missed you this morning."

"Duty calls."

He raised an eyebrow.

"One of my salespeople came down with a bad case of food poisoning and is currently in their room praying to the porcelain god, so I'm here in their stead."

"So it wasn't my charming personality that kept you away?"

"You wish." Naomi bent down and retrieved several

cellophane-wrapped Brooks and Johnson products from underneath her display table.

"I was actually hoping I could steal you away and talk about how Brooks and Johnson might benefit from being part of Knight International."

"Changing tactics, I see," Naomi stated. She began stacking the promotional items on the table. "I have executives that handle that kind of stuff for me. Besides I'm needed here."

"Don't hide behind your work," Lucius responded, glancing around him. "The trade show is going to slow down for lunch anyway, and you have to eat."

Naomi let out a long, beleaguered sigh. "Fine. If it'll get you off my back." She turned and whispered something to her staff.

Lunch at a nearby bistro was not only delicious, but the conversation was less charged than their previous encounters. The change of flow seemed to please Naomi immensely, and she became more at ease during the course of the meal. They talked about politics. The Lakers. Even some charity work she'd started doing. Until eventually the conversation turned to business and the purpose for the lunch.

Lucius explained the reach of Knight International and how having a distribution arm like his would allow Brooks and Johnson to not only be a national phenomenon but an international success. "We could sell B and J products in stores abroad."

"That's all fine and good, Lucius," Naomi responded, "but I'm happy with where the company is right now."

"C'mon, don't tell me you don't have big dreams."

"I do, but I also want to be approachable. I can't do that overseas. I do want a family someday."

Lucius frowned. *Family.* There was a dirty word in

his vocabulary, and one he wasn't altogether fond of. If it wasn't for his grandma Ruby, he wouldn't have any to speak of.

Naomi caught his frown, because she asked, "Are you not close with your family?"

His sat upright in his chair, his shoulders stiff. "No, I'm not."

She must have detected his body language and the note of finality in his tone, which said he didn't wish to continue on the subject, because she dropped it. "I have to get back." Naomi used the napkin in her lap to wipe her mouth.

"So that's it?" Lucius asked. "You're not going to give my proposal any more thought?"

Naomi's eyes narrowed. "I did. I gave you the benefit of lunch and you didn't convince me that the company *I* started, *I* nurtured since infancy, belongs with someone who doesn't even believe in the word *family*. Good day, Lucius."

Lucius stared at Naomi's retreating figure as she went through the revolving doors of the bistro. How had their lunch gone so horribly wrong? He'd been certain he could convince her that Knight International was the next logical step in the evolution of Brooks and Johnson. But not only had he failed at that, he'd also struck a nerve with Naomi when he'd cut down her attempt to open up about his family.

Had he killed any hope that Naomi Brooks would ever give him the time of day again?

"You won't believe who was at the conference," Naomi told Kelsey the next day when she made it back to Long Beach and phoned her friend from her three-bedroom craftsman-style bungalow in Belmont Heights' historic district.

"Who?" Kelsey asked from the other end of the line.

"Lucius Knight," Naomi replied, placing the teakettle on the stove.

"Lucius. Now there's a blast from the past," Kelsey responded. "You haven't spoken of him since college, when you told me about the monumental crush you had on him."

"Yeah, well, that ship has sailed," Naomi responded, turning on the burner. "He's not the bad boy of every teenage girl's fantasy anymore. Instead, he's a pompous, arrogant, conceited jerk."

"Wow!" Kelsey laughed. "I've never heard you speak that way about someone. He must have really gotten your goat."

"He did."

"What happened? Do tell—married women such as myself have to entertain ourselves with sexy single girl stories."

"Wh-what? There's no sex in this story."

"Naomi, chill. I was just kidding. What's gotten into you?" Kelsey inquired. "Did seeing Lucius again really upset you that much?"

Naomi sighed. "Yes—I mean, no."

"Which is it?"

"He was just so smug and confident, saying that I'm attracted to him and that we would eventually sleep together."

Kelsey perked up. "Oh, really? And why would he think that? Did you give him fodder to think he'd have the time of day?"

"No…"

"Hmm…it sounds like you're not being one hundred with me, Naomi. Give up the goods. What happened between you two?"

"All right, all right. We kissed," Naomi answered in a

rush as she leaned back against the counter to wait for the teakettle to boil. "Are you happy now?"

"I would be if you were happy about it. Was he a terribly bad kisser? You know, the ones that slobber all over you, or their tongue is like a lizard darting in and out of your mouth. I used to hate that when I dated. If a man didn't know how to kiss, he got the boot."

Naomi chuckled. "I wish that was the case, but Lucius is far from being a bad kisser. In fact, he's the best kisser I've ever had."

"Is that a fact?"

"It is. And that's also why I have to stay away from him."

"Why? What's wrong with having a little fun? If his reputation is anything to go by, Lucius knows how to treat—or should I say please—a woman. Perhaps Lucius, with his exceptional expertise, is exactly what you need to light your fire."

"Kelsey."

"I'm just being honest. When was your last date? Or relationship?"

"Lucius Knight isn't interested in a relationship with me. He's interested in sleeping with me and buying my company, and not necessarily in that order."

"That's true."

Naomi stood upright. "Why are you agreeing? Did something happen while I was away?"

"His attorney Adam Powell came to see me."

"And why would he do that?" Once the kettle began to whistle, Naomi turned off the burner and poured the boiling water in a teacup.

"To offer me an outrageous sum of money to sell my shares."

"And what did you tell him?"

"No, of course. I would never do that to you, Naomi, and not to our friendship. I promised you I would take time to think through my decision, and I'm doing just that. No amount of money thrown at me would change that."

Naomi released the long sigh she'd been holding in. "Thank you, Kels. I guess I just got a little nervous, is all."

"What I want to know is how would they even know to come to me out of the two of us?"

Naomi rubbed her chin and thought about Kelsey's questions. "Clearly, they were looking for the weak link, and they think you're it, given you're married with a child and another on the way. It's apparent that Lucius doesn't play fair and is looking for my Achilles' heel."

It was just another thing that Naomi was finding she didn't like about the man other than his proclivity against family. Or was it marriage and children? Or all of the above?

Lucius was angry. He'd called and left repeated messages on both Naomi's cell phone and at her office, and yet she continued to ignore him. He'd thought at the very least he and Naomi had formed a pseudofriendship during the couple of days they'd spent in Anaheim.

On their last day together, he'd tried to show her that if they worked as a team, Brooks and Johnson's transition into the Knight International brand would be seamless, but Naomi wanted none of it. Or maybe her ire went deeper? Was she upset because he'd come on so strong about their obvious attraction? Was this her way of telling him to take a hike? If so, she was wrong on that score.

Lucius never gave up on something he wanted. He wanted Naomi. *And* her company.

Since returning from Anaheim nearly a week ago, he'd dived back into work full force, trying to erase the memory of the curly-haired beauty from his mind, but he couldn't. He would daydream about what it had been like to kiss her in that elevator, and his dreams went farther into what would have happened if that door had *never* opened.

He imagined taking Naomi against the wall. He'd have stripped her of any clothes, spread her legs and licked her until she begged him to make love to her. Only then would he have pushed down his jeans and plunged deep inside her wet heat. He knew she'd been wet for him. The way she'd squirmed in his arms had told him exactly what he'd needed to know. Naomi was as hot for him as he was for her.

He just had to get the woman to admit it.

She was as stubborn as a mule, and this last week had proved so. But he wasn't going to take this lying down. He was going to make Naomi acknowledge that not only was Brooks and Johnson a good fit for his brand, but more importantly, Naomi was a good fit for him.

Chapter 5

Naomi called it quits. It had been a long day. A late one, actually—she'd stayed well past 6:00 p.m. But it had been worth it. Today's think tank meeting had yielded some great ideas for the product line.

She waved at the security guard manning the entrance to the building as she made her way outside. One of the perks of having her own company was she got a prime parking space right outside the building rather than having to use the parking garage in the rear.

Naomi pushed open the glass door and breathed in the cool night air. She quickly buttoned up her peacoat and glanced up at the sky. Fall was here, and it felt good.

Or at least so she thought, until her gaze lowered and she saw Lucius standing outside a limousine several feet away.

"Join me for dinner?"

"I don't think that's a good idea, Lucius." Naomi started toward her Audi A5 coupe that was parked several feet away, but Lucius rose from where he'd been leaning and blocked her path.

"Please."

Naomi was sure Lucius never used that word often. He was used to issuing commands and people followed them, but he wasn't doing that now. Her head told her to keep walking, but instead, she walked toward the limousine. Lucius reached across and opened the door, and Naomi climbed inside. She scooted onto the plush leather passenger cushions. The limo was well furnished, but then again, this was how the rich and famous lived, right?

Lucius slid in beside her, and when he did, Naomi swallowed tightly and her pulse skittered alarmingly at being so close to Lucius. "And where are we going?"

"You'll see," Lucius said. "Just sit back and relax." He pressed on the intercom button and said to the driver, "You know the destination."

Lucius didn't like that Naomi was uneasy around him. Her guard was up and he wanted to get through to her, get her to see that he had a solid plan for Brooks and Johnson. An added benefit would be her becoming putty in his hands when he seduced her.

He did not, however, like the look of fear in her eyes, and so he engaged her in conversation. "You can stop fearing for your safety, Naomi. I won't harm you."

He watched her shoulders visibly sag. "I wanted to speak with you, but you didn't really give me much choice since you've ignored my calls.

"Perhaps there was nothing you had to say that I would be interested in."

"Ah." His index finger circled her face. "There's the feisty Naomi I know and like."

"Flattery will get you nowhere."

"No?" Lucius said. "Let's see if that holds true at the end of the night."

"You think you'll make it that long?"

"Until you've listened again to my pitch. After that—" he shrugged "—I'm going to guess that you won't want to."

Naomi folded her arms across her chest. "You don't know that."

"I know that you're curious as to why I contacted you and why I waited for you tonight."

"You waited for me?" Naomi's brow furrowed.

Lucius didn't speak, he just let Naomi marinate on that thought while he reached for the bottle of champagne that was chilling in the bucket beside him. "An aperitif?"

"I suppose. I'm not much of a drinker. So why is it I only seem to drink around you?"

"Perhaps it's a way for you to release your inhibitions."

That comment brought a frown from Naomi, and she turned to silently stare out the window while Lucius uncorked and poured each of them a glass of champagne. "Here." He held out the flute to her. She accepted but didn't look at him.

"Naomi, this night will turn out far better if you perhaps acknowledge that you don't dislike me as much as you protest."

Her head spun around, and she glared at him underneath mascara-coated lashes. He noticed that she had more makeup on than he'd seen her wear on prior occasions. She was more put together, in a black and tweed dress that reached her knees and black pumps. Lucius didn't like this stuffy Naomi. He much preferred the natural, more organic Naomi, who was more comfortable in jeans and a tank top.

She finally spoke. "I—I don't dislike you."

"What then?"

"As I said before, you're arrogant, but I also find you untrustworthy and unscrupulous."

"Unscrupulous? That's a strong word."

"Did you or did you not send your attorney to speak

with my partner, Kelsey, while I was in Anaheim so you could double-team us?"

Lucius sipped his champagne. So she knew about that? No wonder she'd ignored his calls.

"Are you going to deny it?" she asked when he didn't answer.

"No, that would be dishonest," he responded curtly.

"Which proves my point." Naomi took another gulp of champagne. "I can't trust you."

He turned to face her. "Do you want to?"

"Wh-what?"

"You heard the question. Why does my behavior bother you so, Naomi?" His steady gaze bored into her in silent expectation.

"I don't care one way or the other."

"Who's lying now?" he asked quietly.

She stared wordlessly at him, and Lucius knew it was time to tell her the truth. "C'mon, Naomi, did you really think I'm that callous that I don't remember the awkward fifteen-year-old girl that used to follow me around in high school?"

Naomi's entire face flushed, and he could see he'd hit the nail on the head. She had remembered him. She gulped down the remainder of her champagne.

"So you know who I am." She set her empty flute in the cup holder. "What of it?"

"So I know that you used to harbor a schoolgirl crush on me way back when. And I know that I thought you could be cute if you'd just take off those stupid glasses, get some better facial products, do something with your hair and stop trying to hide your figure. It seems I was right on all fronts."

Naomi sucked in a sharp breath. He could see he'd embarrassed her, but he wasn't above using sentimentality to get his way. He leaned back slightly so he could assess her frankly. "Your skin is clear, which I'm sure is due to Brooks and Johnson products. You wear contacts now, and your hair, well—" he reached out to finger several tendrils "—natural looks good on you. And as for the figure…" His gaze lazily roved over her entire body. "I like everything I see."

"I'm so glad you approve," Naomi replied flippantly.

"Don't be upset." Lucius scooted closer to Naomi, and this time she didn't move away from him. "It was a compliment." He stroked the soft skin of her cheek. "You've turned into a beautiful woman. A woman I am very much attracted to."

His gaze immediately went to her lips. Lips he wanted to kiss. Had been craving to kiss since the elevator in Anaheim. He glanced upward to her neck and could see her pulse quickening. Gone was the embarrassment of a moment ago, and in its place he could feel the electricity he'd felt since they'd met.

He bent his head and claimed her lips. He kissed her nice and slow so she didn't push him away. He needed her to acquiesce. At first she remained still, but as his mouth covered hers hungrily, Naomi gave up the pretense she didn't want him and her arms snaked around his neck.

Lucius groaned as he broke the barrier of her lips and teeth and she allowed his tongue to surge inside her mouth. He left no part of her mouth untouched. He tasted every nook and crevice of its honeyed interior, but what was most surprising was how he felt while doing it. Instead of making her burn for him, he was burning for her. His hands threaded through her hair as he devoured her mouth. He had an aching need to forget all semblance of romance and just bury himself deep inside her right now in the back of this limo.

Fate was on her side, because the limo came to an abrupt stop, causing him to slowly ease away from Naomi. When he glanced in her direction, Naomi's hair was tousled and her lips looked swollen, because he'd thoroughly made love to them.

Naomi used her fingers to comb her hair back into place. She didn't say a word when the driver came around and opened her door. She just disembarked and waited for him on the sidewalk.

Lucius exited right behind her and reached for her hand, but Naomi ignored it and walked inside without him.

Naomi stared at Lucius after they'd been seated by the hostess and placed their order with a very supercilious waiter. In the limo, he'd told her that he was very aware of her when they were in high school. "Why did you say it? To get me off track from the real reason you're so desperate to contact me'?"

"Say what?"

"That you found me cute back in high school. You said it to disarm me, so I'd let down my guard. Very sneaky, Lucius."

"I meant it."

Naomi snorted. There was no way a man or boy as good-looking as Lucius had found an awkward outcast like her remotely attractive.

"You don't believe me?" Lucius watched her across the rim of his glass. "Of course you don't, because I'm ruthless and can't be trusted. Is everything so black-and-white to you, Naomi? Or don't you see in shades of color?"

"I see you very clearly, Lucius. And I won't be played."

"Yes, I'm relentless when I want something, but one doesn't negate the other. It doesn't mean that I don't find you desirable and want you in my bed."

"There!" She pointed her index finger at him again. "You're doing it again. Trying to seduce me."

"I don't have to try." Lucius leaned back in his chair. "I think that was pretty obvious from the way you responded in the limo."

Naomi didn't answer and reached for her water glass. All of a sudden, she felt very thirsty. Perhaps it was Lucius's hungry gaze that was making her parched. She drank liberally, giving herself time to gather her thoughts.

"You have a way with women, Lucius. Everyone knows it. And I know it. It's not surprising that you could garner a reaction from me. I imagine you're quite skilled in that department."

"I am," Lucius said. "Skilled in the bedroom and out of it. And that's why you and your partner shouldn't toss aside the deal my team has presented. It's more than fair."

"We're not interested."

The waiter returned at that moment with the expensive bottle of wine Lucius ordered. He poured Naomi a taste, and once she'd sipped and nodded in agreement, he filled her glass and Lucius's.

Once he'd gone, Lucius wasted no time getting back to the topic at hand. "Am I the reason you're not giving this offer credence? Are you doing this just to spite me?"

"Spite you?" Naomi's head fell back with laughter. "You give yourself a lot of credit, Lucius. There are other wolves just like you waiting to pounce in the wings." She wasn't about to tell him that her partnership with Kelsey was on rocky ground because motherhood and family had become central to Kelsey. And that *she* might be interested in his offer. "But I'll tell them the exact same thing I'm telling you—I'm never giving up controlling interest in my company."

He watched her warily, as if he was assessing her answer. Naomi sensed that he wanted to say more, but he didn't.

The waiter returned with their entrées of succulent shrimp risotto and spiced duck. They both indulged in the delicious dishes in contemplative silence before Lucius took the conversation down a different path.

"It's clear, Naomi, we've reached an impasse on all talk of business for tonight, but that doesn't mean the evening has to be a bust. So can we toast to having an enjoyable evening?"

Naomi thought about it a moment. She didn't know how she was going to do that. The wariness she felt for Lucius was armor for her to deflect the attraction she felt. Without it, she was forced to admit to herself that she enjoyed his company. Having removed his jacket, he looked gorgeous in the white button-down shirt that was open at the collar and black slacks. His hair was trimmed so that the wave in it was noticeable. His deeply set dark eyes stared directly across the table at her, waiting for her answer.

"Yes." She held up her flute reluctantly. "I suppose I can do that."

An irrepressible grin slid over his incredibly full lips.

Naomi swallowed. It was going to be a long night.

Lucius was happy with how the evening progressed between him and Naomi. They'd adjourned from the restaurant to sit beside each other—Lucius on one side of a padded wicker love seat and Naomi far away on the other—on the terrace outside and enjoy the crisp fall evening with an after-dinner drink. The terrace was dimly lit by thin strings of light and strategically placed candles.

Lucius regarded her silently.

Sure, his interest in her company had been met with

outright hostility, but once they'd agreed to put their differences on the shelf, he found Naomi a breath of fresh air.

There was no pretense with her. What you saw was what you got. She wasn't like other women, who, once they found out who he was or how much he was worth, were eager to fawn all over him or want him to buy them things. Naomi Brooks was nothing like them. In fact, she couldn't care less about things. She cared about people.

It was evident in the way she passionately spoke about her family. Throughout the course of the night, he'd learned her parents were still together after thirty-five years of marriage and she had a brother and a sister whom she loved dearly. Then there was her volunteerism—Naomi was involved in several charitable organizations that supported helping children and fighting breast cancer.

Lucius wasn't sure he'd ever met anyone quite like Naomi. She was more selfless than anyone he'd ever known.

"What?" Naomi was staring back at him.

He blinked several times. "I'm sorry, say again?"

"Am I boring you?" she inquired. "I know I'm not like some of the actresses and models you've dated, who I'm sure indulge in more titillating conversation."

Lucius laughed broadly. "Boring? Ha. That's the last adjective I would use to describe you, Naomi. I was just musing on the difference between you and my usual companions."

Naomi eyed him suspiciously. "Am I really all that different?"

"You've certainly changed from the nerdy tomboy in baggy jeans and plaid shirts," Lucius countered.

"And you?" She eyed him in return. "You're just as dangerous as you were as a teenager, which is why I must be cautious of you, Lucius Knight, despite how charming you're being." She glanced down at her watch. "We should call it a night. I have a busy day in the morning." She rose from the love seat.

Lucius hated for the night to end. He wanted to spend more time with her, but he would have to bide his time. "Of course." He stood. "Shall we?" He offered her his arm.

At first, he thought she wouldn't take it, but she must have realized she was out of danger at least for tonight, so she accepted his proffered arm as they walked to the elevators.

Several minutes later, they were back in his limousine and driving to her office so she could pick up her car. She was quiet on the way back, deep in thought. He wanted to know what was on her mind and why she had a concerned wrinkle on her forehead, but he doubted she would reveal her troubles to him. Why? Because she didn't trust him.

Lucius didn't know why it bothered him, but it did. He wanted her to trust him.

They made it back to the Brooks and Johnson building too quickly, in his opinion. Before Naomi could reach for the door, he used the intercom button to tell the driver he would need a minute.

Naomi turned to him in confusion.

"I really enjoyed our evening together," Lucius stated.

She looked relieved, as if she thought he was going to pounce on her. "So did I." She reached for the handle, but Lucius grasped her hand. "Lucius, don't…"

"Naomi…" He used his index finger to turn her head to face him. He glanced down at her mouth. Her lips were slightly parted, and he watched when her tongue darted out to lick them nervously. That was his undoing.

He reached for her and dipped his head to taste her mouth. Once, then twice before he began to devour her.

* * *

All the air in Naomi's lungs left her at Lucius's electric kiss. Every cell in her came alive, and her heart hammered loudly in her chest. Damn it! She'd tried to get out of the limo as quickly as she could without being rude, but he'd done it again. He was kissing her with no mercy until she had no choice but to return his kiss.

He raked his tongue across her top and bottom lips until she parted them for his tongue. His arms vised around her body, pulling her close enough and positioning her underneath him. That's when he began kissing her deeply and so passionately, Naomi's head spun.

He made her feel alive, desired. No other man had ever made her feel like this. And she hadn't known that she could. He tore his mouth from hers long enough so his tongue could glide a wet path along the base of her throat and upward to her neck. And when his teeth made their way to her ear and he began tonguing it, Naomi moaned gently from underneath him as a wild rush of emotions began to rip through her system.

Good God! What the man was doing to her was making her wet between her thighs.

"Naomi…" Lucius groaned her name as his teeth and tongue left her ear to snake their way down. He pushed her peacoat aside so he could mold her breasts through the tweed fabric of her dress.

Naomi could feel them turn into pebbles beneath his skilled touch. She wanted to feel not just his hands but his mouth *on her.* She didn't resist when his hands roamed over her hip, thigh and leg. She didn't stop him when she felt the hem of her dress being lifted. She could only feel.

When Lucius's fingers reached the thin, lacy fabric of her bikini panties and pushed them aside to cover her warm cleft, Naomi shuddered. He touched her intimately, and Naomi let out a long hiss.

"Look at me." Naomi heard Lucius through the haze of emotions whirling through her.

She glanced up at him as his finger slid inside her. The glittering shine of hunger in his eyes was unmistakable as he stroked her in and out, over and over again until Naomi was a quivering mass of nerve endings.

"Come for me, Naomi." His fingers slowed their movements as they played with her swollen clit, time after torturous time, going deeper.

"I—I…" Naomi couldn't think. Lucius had her on the verge of coming. It was a mixture of ecstasy and agony rolled into one. She was panting for more, and when Lucius placed a second finger inside her and played her like a violin, Naomi broke, splintering into a thousand pieces.

She closed her eyes and waited for her breathing to return to normal. She couldn't look at him now. She was too embarrassed that he had just made her lose all control in the back of a limo. She was sure he was used to doing this kind of thing all the time with all sorts of women, but she wasn't one of them. And she wouldn't be used for his satisfaction. She had to put a stop to it.

Lucius was nibbling on Naomi's delicious neck when he felt her resistance. He stopped immediately and pulled them both upward. "What is it?" He searched her face for a sign of what had changed between them.

That's when he saw the tears in her eyes. "Naomi, I'm sorry…"

"Don't." She held up her hand. "I was an equal participant."

"Then what's wrong?" He was confused. Naomi had

enjoyed that kiss as much as he had. He'd felt it. She'd felt it. And she'd had an orgasm. Was that what scared her?

"I can't do this with you, Lucius. I should have never allowed this evening to continue after that first kiss," she said as she began rearranging her mussed clothing. He'd very much enjoyed finally having the opportunity to touch her body and feel her respond to him.

"Clearly I'm not immune to you," Naomi continued. "So I'm going to have to keep my distance." She reached for the handle. "And I suggest you do the same."

Before Lucius could react, she'd jumped out of the limousine. "Naomi!" He rushed toward the door, but she was racing to her car and was inside before he made it out of the vehicle.

Lucius watched as she started her car and sped away.

Slowly he slid back into the limo. Why was she running from him? He'd rather thought they were off to a good start. He'd hoped to convince her to spend the night with him, but that wasn't going to happen tonight—or any other night in the foreseeable future, if Naomi had anything to say about.

She'd been right when she said she wasn't immune to him, and Lucius intended to use it to his advantage. He wanted Naomi more than he'd wanted a woman in a long time. He would just have to wear down her defenses until she saw they could make beautiful music together.

Chapter 6

Images of Lucius kissing her in the back of the limo while his fingers were deep inside her flooded Naomi's mind as she drove to her parents' for dinner on Sunday. She was grateful for some semblance of normalcy after the crazy week she'd endured.

Seeing Lucius again after all these years, spending time with him and then finally that last passion-crazed night in which she'd made out with him in the limo not once, but twice, was troubling. She'd tried unsuccessfully to get him out of her mind, but he kept coming back like a boomerang. The way he'd kissed her, the way he tasted, the way he'd made her come with *his fingers*!

That night when she'd gotten home, she'd been mortified that she'd allowed their encounter to unravel. A kiss she could blow off, but she'd allowed him to take liberties with her body. To touch her. Make her orgasm. And what made matters worse was that now her body craved more. Her traitorous body wanted to feel him buried deep inside her, wanted to feel that gut-clenching, overwhelming sensation she'd felt when he'd made her come.

Naomi blinked several times as she pulled into her

parents' driveway next to her brother's minivan and her sister's scooter. It was bad, really bad. She was developing feelings for Lucius Knight again when she should be on her guard. The man didn't just want her. He wanted her company, too.

Turning off the engine, Naomi reached for the apple pie she'd made earlier that afternoon and exited the vehicle. She used her key and entered her parents' house moments later.

"Thanks, sweetie." Her mother, Ava Brooks, a petite woman with Naomi's same naturally riotous curls, greeted her in the hall with a kiss and relieved her of the pie. "You know you didn't have to make anything."

Naomi shrugged as she removed her jacket and hung it up on the coatrack in the foyer. "I know, but I wanted to. Where's everybody?"

"You know your dad and brother are in front of the tube watching football. Audrey's in the kitchen."

Naomi waved at her sister-in-law, Audrey, and rushed toward her father sitting in his recliner in the adjoining family room. "Dad." She gave him a squeeze around the neck.

"How's my baby girl?" Benjamin Brooks asked, glancing up at her with eyes as dark as midnight. With her caramel coloring and small frame, Naomi favored her mother, while her father had chocolate skin and a football player's build and was six feet tall.

"Just fine, Daddy." Naomi smiled as she came over to give her brother, Timothy, a hug.

"What's up, sis?" Timothy said, barely taking his eyes off the screen, not wanting to miss a play.

"Where's Gemma?" Naomi glanced around for her sister. As the youngest in the family at twenty-four, Gemma was the baby, but she was also the troublemaker and resident screwup. Naomi suspected by the time her parents got to Gemma they'd lightened up their parenting style dramatically. If Timothy or Naomi had done half the things Gemma did, they would have gotten in trouble or been kicked out of the house.

"Outside, I think," her father said. "Wanna beer?" He motioned to the cooler he kept by his side on game day.

"Sure." Her father opened the cooler and handed her a can. "Thanks." She popped the top and left them to find her sister.

She slid the door next to the family room open and found Gemma on the patio whispering on the phone. "Hey, Gemma," Naomi said from the doorway.

Startled, Gemma glanced up. "Oh, hey. How long you been here?"

"Not long. What's going on?"

Gemma placed her hand over the receiver. "Wrapping up a call. Can we talk later?"

"See you inside." Naomi wondered what she was up to but went inside anyway. She couldn't clean up any more of Gemma's problems. Her sister couldn't keep a steady job, but it was time Gemma stood on her own two feet.

She returned to the kitchen, where her mother and Audrey were making dinner. "Need any help?" Naomi asked, sitting on a bar stool at the breakfast bar.

"No, we have it under control," her mother replied. "So why don't you tell us what's new with you, such as the wealthy businessman who's interested in acquiring Brooks and Johnson? I ran into Kelsey's mom and she mentioned it."

Naomi rolled her eyes. She wanted to strangle Kelsey's mom. The last thing she wanted to do today was discuss Lucius Knight, but it looked like fate was not on her side.

"Yeah, actually I went to high school with him back in the day."

Her mother stopped stirring whatever she was cooking in the pot to glance at her. "Really? Were you friends?"

We definitely were not friends, Naomi thought. "No, I didn't really know him."

"And now he wants your company?"

Naomi nodded. "I'm not selling."

"Kelsey's mom told me that she might be," her mother replied.

Naomi took a swig of beer. "With the new baby, she's considering it, but I told her to let me know before she makes a final decision so I can buy her out."

"Can you afford to do that?" her brother asked. Timothy leaned against the breakfast bar behind her and reached across into the popcorn bowl sitting on the bar. He tossed a few kernels in his mouth. "You would need to come up with a lot of capital, and that's after you'd finally cleared all your debt with the IPO. It wouldn't be advisable."

Naomi knew this was right up her accountant brother's alley. "I don't know," she answered honestly. It was the first time she was admitting she might have a hard time raising that kind of money.

"Perhaps you need to give the offer some thought as well," her mother chimed in. "I mean, what you've done is amazing, but are you really ready to take B and J to the next level?"

"Thanks a lot, Mom." Naomi took another swig of beer.

"I'm sure your mom didn't mean anything by it." Her father came to her mother's rescue as he joined everyone in the kitchen. "*We* both believe in you, Naomi—always have. We wouldn't have given you the start-up money if we didn't."

Her parents and Kelsey's had loaned them the money

for the initial investment in Brooks and Johnson until they could pay them back. Naomi would always be grateful for their help, but this was something she would have to figure out on her own.

"I wish you guys would help me out like you helped Naomi," Gemma said, closing the sliding door to the pool.

"Of course, it's always about you, Gemma," Timothy said, glancing in her direction. "We were talking about Naomi."

Gemma made a face at him, and they all laughed.

"Dinner is ready," her mother stated. "Now, how about you guys help me and Audrey bring everything to the dining room?"

Ten minutes later, the entire Brooks family was seated at the dining room table. Benjamin said grace before they dug into the roast and sides Ava and Audrey had prepared.

"Looks good, Ma," Timothy commented.

Ava smiled. "Thank you, baby."

"So." Timothy turned to Naomi, who was seated on one side while his wife sat opposite him with Gemma. "Who is the businessman that's interested in B and J?"

Naomi had hoped the conversation was over. No such luck. "Lucius Knight."

"Knight, did you say? Isn't he that guy you used to fawn over in high school?" Timothy inquired.

Naomi blushed. "I did not fawn."

Gemma chuckled from across the table. "Liar. Look at how she's blushing." She pointed in Naomi's direction.

Naomi shifted uncomfortably in her seat as everyone at the table stared at her. "Fine. I may have had a crush on him, but for Christ's sake, I'm a grown woman now."

"Have you seen Lucius lately?" Gemma asked. "He was recently featured in *Black Enterprise* magazine as a rising star in the business world because of his shrewdness in takeovers. *And* he's simply gorgeous."

Naomi cast her eyes upward. Trust her sister to keep track of these things. "I hadn't noticed."

"So you've seen him?" Gemma picked up on what she hadn't said.

"Yes, I met him at the conference in Anaheim." Naomi figured that tidbit would be enough to appease her family.

"And was he as sexy as all the photos?" Gemma inquired.

"Gemma!" her father cautioned her sternly.

"C'mon, Dad. He's a known womanizer. I'm just asking if he's made a play for Naomi."

"This topic of conversation is extremely inappropriate," their mother scolded Gemma.

Gemma shrugged.

"If Gemma's right," Timothy said from her side, "then it might be wise to start reviewing your finances to be sure you can raise the capital if Kelsey wants to sell. A man like Lucius might not have any scruples about driving a wedge between longtime friends and business partners."

Naomi turned to stare at her brother. He had a point. She'd never thought about just how far Lucius might go to get what he wanted.

"If you want, I can help you look over your books and your finances to see what we can come up with."

"I would love that, Tim."

"Consider it done."

"Then let's move on to a new topic," her father said as he gave her a wink. She was thankful that he'd sensed her unease and she could get off the family hot seat, because Naomi suspected that she was far from out of the fire. In fact, she suspected that now that Lucius smelled victory, he would keep coming on strong.

* * *

Lucius would have loved to focus on business, Naomi or anything else other than deal with his mother, but he'd promised Grandma Ruby. His mother had already been back for a week and hadn't taken kindly to the fact that he hadn't spoken to her on the phone or come for a visit.

What did she expect, for Christ's sake?

She'd been MIA for most of his life. And just because she wanted to play the mommy role now did not mean he was about to roll over.

When Lucius arrived early that evening to Jocelyn Turner's penthouse, which she kept for her visits to Long Beach, she was happy to see him.

"Lucius, my darling." Rather than a hug, his mother kissed him on both cheeks and ushered him inside. "I'm so glad you finally decided to visit me."

Lucius heard the derisive note in her voice as he headed for the formal living room. He didn't intend on staying long. Time with his mother always got under his skin, and he wanted to keep it to a minimum. "I have a busy schedule, Jocelyn. Perhaps if you would schedule these visits I could put you on my calendar." He walked over to the wet bar on the far side of the room. He took the top off the decanter of scotch and poured himself a drink.

"I'm your mother, Lucius. I shouldn't have to be put on your calendar." She followed him in the room with her arms folded across her chest.

Lucius glanced backward at her. She was dressed in a silk lounge set that clearly was designer and quite costly. Her shoulder-length hair was in a loose chignon, and several expensive baubles adorned her neck, ears and fingers. Whoever she was seeing was quite wealthy and kept her in jewels. And had for years.

As for her face, his mother was a stunningly beautiful

woman. He'd inherited her smooth café au lait–colored skin and dark brown eyes. A flaw could not be seen on her impeccable complexion, and her figure was just as impressive. Even at fifty-four, Jocelyn Turner was still a head turner.

Lucius sipped his scotch before responding to her last comment. "You haven't earned the right to make unannounced visits. I owe you nothing."

"I'm still your mother, Lucius."

"Only when you seem to remember it and aren't traipsing the globe and hanging as an adornment on some rich man's arm."

"Lucius!" His mother covered her mouth with her hands and rushed out of the room and onto the terrace several feet away.

As soon as he said aloud the words he'd been thinking, he regretted them. Why did Jocelyn bring out the worst in him? Ever since he was a little kid, he'd been angered by her refusal to tell him who his father was. And because of it, he'd hardened his heart toward her. So much so that whenever they were within a few feet of each other, his claws came out.

Putting down his drink on the table, Lucius joined her on the terrace. He placed his hands on her shoulders, and they sagged at his nearness. "I'm sorry. I shouldn't have said that."

She patted his hands and turned around to face him. Her eyelashes were wet with tears. "Why do you despise me so? Haven't I given you everything?"

Lucius swallowed. He hated to see the hurt in her eyes, but he also wouldn't act as if she hadn't kept the truth from him his entire life. She was no mother of the year. "You haven't given me the one thing I want most, Mother."

He didn't use the title often, but in this instance he was trying to make amends as best he could.

"You know I can't do that."

And just as quickly the sentiment passed and Lucius stepped away from her. "You mean you *won't*."

"It's not the same."

"Like hell it isn't," Lucius stated. "How long will you continue to keep me in the dark? My whole life? What if I have a family of my own someday? Don't I have the right to know who I came from? My genetic makeup?" His investigation into his paternity had included researching men in his mother's past. He'd even researched men with the last name Knight, but had come up empty.

"Family?" She spun around to face him. "Have you gone and gotten one of the social climbers you associate with pregnant?"

"Of course you would think that," Lucius responded with an eye roll, "but I wouldn't want to end up like you. I suppose that's why you wish you'd never had me."

He turned to look out over the city. The sun would be setting soon.

He felt Jocelyn's hand on his arm, tugging him around to face her. "I've never regretted having you, Lucius. I love you. But I do worry about the women you choose to spend time with. Some of them would love to trap a man of your considerable wealth into a loveless marriage, and it would cost you a fortune to get rid of them. I would never want that for you."

Lucius regarded her quizzically. "Is that why my father never left his wife for you? Because he chose his money over love?" His mother turned away and didn't answer him. It seemed she'd been talking from personal experience. "I'm right, aren't I?"

"You don't understand, Lucius."

His fingers curved around her arm. "I don't because you've never helped me to understand. You've always kept the truth from me. What can it matter now? I'm a grown man. I don't need or want anything from my father. I just want to know who I am."

She stared at him with fresh tears in her ears. "I'm sorry, Lucius."

Lucius frowned and clenched his teeth. Yet again, as soon as he got too close, she shut him out. "So am I, because I can't continue to do this."

"What do you mean?"

"I won't be coming to visit you again."

"You can't mean that."

"I do mean it. I'm tired of playing this merry-go-round with you, Jocelyn. Either you tell me the truth of my parentage or you can consider yourself childless."

"You're giving me an ultimatum?"

"Damn right. So what's it going to be?" He folded his arms.

She shook her head as if she couldn't believe it was happening. "Please don't do this, Lucius." She rushed off the terrace and back into the living room, where she began pacing the floor.

"Do what?"

She stopped pacing momentarily to say, "Make me choose."

"I would think the choice is pretty clear. You can choose to have a relationship with me, *your son*. Or you can choose to continue to be *his* side piece. Always living in the shadows. Never his top priority. Never coming first."

She turned away to face the mantel that held several pictures of Lucius at various stages of his life. Stages she'd missed. There was one of him in his Boy Scout uniform with his grandma Ruby, another when he played football during the seventh grade and another with him in his cap and gown standing next to her and Ruby. Jocelyn had managed to make his high school graduation.

"Lucius, I know you can't understand this, but I vowed I would never reveal your father's identity, and I've honored it all these years. It hasn't been easy, I promise you that. Each and every time you've asked me, begged me—" her broke voice "—pleaded with me, I've wanted to tell you, but it was my choice to have you, not his and I have never regretted giving birth to you. My biggest regret is that I haven't been the best mother and can't give you the one thing you want most."

Lucius was stunned, and tears bit at his eyes, but he refused to let her see she'd finally broken him. He didn't know why, but he'd always held out the hope that one day she would tell him the truth. One day, she would put *him* first, but now he realized how foolish he'd been. She would never do that. He would always be last on her list of her priorities.

Lucius would never understand it. He walked toward the wet bar and chugged the scotch remaining in the glass. "Then consider this the last time we'll meet." He placed the glass back on the bar and strode toward the door.

She reached him at the door and tugged his arm. "Lucius, please forgive me. I'm so sorry."

He shrugged her away. "I'm finished with you. And this time for good."

Chapter 7

Lucius could use another stiff drink. It was usually how he felt after an encounter with his mother, but instead he chose a long walk on the beach to clear his mind. The sun in shades of red, orange and yellow was already setting in a half-moon shape on the horizon. Plus, it was an unseasonably mild evening, and he could use the fresh air. He discarded his jacket in the car and removed his shoes and socks, rolled up his trousers and headed to the ocean.

Why did he always wish for the impossible? Jocelyn was never going to tell him who his father was. She was always going to act like she was the put-upon, long-suffering mother and he was the ungrateful son. He shouldn't play into the role, but Jocelyn had a way of bringing out the worst in him.

Ever since he could remember, he'd been angry with her for a life denied to him. It had hurt the most when he was younger, when other little boys would talk about their fathers, or Father's Day would come around and his would be MIA. He would long for a tall, strong man to come and scoop him up in his arms and take him away from it all, but that day never came. And with each passing year, Lucius became angrier with Jocelyn for keeping the secret.

Lucius was kicking pebbles with his bare feet when he saw a figure in the distance.

Could it be?

It couldn't be.

As the shapely figure in denim capris and an oversize sweater continued to walk toward him, Lucius realized he was right. It was Naomi.

Naomi stared in disbelief at the tall, imposing man striding toward her with a purposeful walk. Of all the odds, on all the days, why did Lucius Knight have to end up on her beach now? She'd come for a little space and peace of mind after the Brooks family dinner had ended with her on the hot seat.

Her family had been extremely curious about Lucius, his intentions and her former feelings for the man. Though lately, those feelings weren't all that former. Since his return to her life, Naomi hadn't been able to get the man off her mind. He had a way of stirring up emotions and passions in her that she thought had been buried.

She continued walking and only stopped when they were a few feet from each other. Lucius was wearing a frown.

"What are you doing out here?" he inquired. "It'll be getting dark soon and you shouldn't be walking on a beach alone at night. It isn't safe."

Naomi laughed and began walking backward. "Actually, I'm probably a lot safer than when I'm with you."

"What's that supposed to mean?"

Naomi shrugged and turned around to go back toward her car.

"Wait up!" Lucius ran after her. He fell into step beside

her. Instead of commenting on her statement, they walked together in silence. Eventually he asked again. "What are you doing out here *alone*?"

She hazarded a glance at him. "Same as you, I suspect. Needed some solitary time."

"Rough night?"

Naomi shook her brown curls. "No, I was with my family."

"Sounds like a rough night."

"Oh, that's right, because you don't believe in family," Naomi replied, stopping in the sand to turn and stare at him. "Well, it isn't like that for me, Lucius. I love my family. They were just a bit more opinionated than I would have cared for tonight. And it gave me food for thought, is all." She started walking again, and Lucius followed by her side.

"Hmm…" he murmured. "Care to share?"

"Not really. And why are you out here alone on the beach? I would think you could find any number of obliging females to make a *From Here to Eternity* movie scene come to life."

He turned to stare blankly at her and paused midstride. "Excuse me?"

Naomi laughed and stopped abruptly. "You're not much on old black-and-white movies, huh?"

Lucius chuckled. "No, I'm not. What's it about?"

"It's an oldie but goodie. It's about three soldiers and stars Hollywood legends like Burt Lancaster, Montgomery Clift and Sinatra. All the action takes place in Hawaii before the attack on Pearl Harbor. Deborah Kerr is the love interest and has an affair with Burt Lancaster's character. They share a steamy moment on the beach in the sand and surf."

"And would *you* like one of those Hollywood moments?" Lucius teased as he smiled down at her.

She hated that even now Lucius looked just as sexy to her as he had all those years ago in high school. Except now he seemed more relaxed and less dangerous than he had in all their other encounters.

Naomi grinned broadly. "Wouldn't you like to know."

She turned on her heel and began walking again.

"Why can't you keep still?"

"Like you, I came for a walk, and we keep stopping."

"Would you prefer to be alone?"

Naomi glanced at him but didn't stop walking. "No, I don't mind the company."

"Good, because I'm not leaving you out here where anyone could harm you."

"How gallant of you."

"Don't be smart—" he wagged a finger at her "—or I'll throw you in the surf and give you your *From Here to Eternity* moment. I'll just bet that would quiet that mouth of yours."

Naomi's eyes grew large. He wouldn't dare. Would he? She stared in his deeply set dark brown eyes. And the answer was emphatic—yes, he would.

Lucius loved teasing Naomi and watching her get all riled up. There was a bright-eyed innocence to her that he found refreshing. He hadn't found it in the beautiful models and actresses he'd dated. He couldn't go beneath the surface with them, but with Naomi he could. Hell, even wanted to.

"What's on your mind, slick?" Naomi asked.

"Slick?"

"Yeah," Naomi laughed. "Kind of suits you."

"Yeah, well, it sounds like you don't think I'm genuine," Lucius responded, and for some reason the thought bothered him. He wanted Naomi to know that he had feelings, real emotions. He wasn't made of stone. An evening with his mother had shown him that.

Naomi turned to stare at him questioningly. "I'm sorry. I didn't mean to offend you."

"You didn't." He bent down, snatched up a rock and threw it into the surf.

"Hmm…kind of sounds like I did, and I'm sorry. What brings you out on an evening stroll, Lucius?"

He shrugged. He didn't want to talk about himself or his reunion with his mother and their nerve-racking fight. He was tired of the same ole song.

"You can talk to me. Maybe I can help."

Lucius glanced back at her. "There's nothing you can do to help," he responded, "except help me forget."

"And how would I do that?"

Her question was all innocence, but the idea of how she could make him forget was not lost on him. He could think of a number of wicked things he'd love to do to her right now on the beach. How he would enjoy nothing better than to strip her naked and take her in the surf, plunging deep inside her as the waves crashed around them.

"Hmm… I see your mind is in the gutter," Naomi said. "And here I was thinking we were finally getting someplace."

He frowned. "We are. And if you must know, I was upset after seeing my mother."

"Why would that upset you?"

"It's a long story, but suffice to say she and I don't see eye to eye. Never have, and that's never gonna change."

Naomi reached out and touched his bare arm. A spark of electricity jolted straight through him, and he turned to her. Her eyes lowered, and he was sure she'd felt it, but he didn't act on it. Instead, he continued. "I wish I had a family like yours, Naomi. You're close and actually enjoy spending time with each other."

"Yes. We do. I don't know what I'd do without them. They're my support system."

"You're lucky. Not all of us get to have that."

"Wait a second, what about your grandmother? I thought I read somewhere that she's been a big part of your life."

Lucius smiled when he turned to Naomi. So she'd been reading up about him. It gave him hope that Naomi was more interested than she let on. "Yes, she is, but it's not the same as having a mother and father who love you. Siblings. God—" he shook his head "—I remember being a little kid and wishing I had a brother or sister. Someone I could talk to or lean on, but there was no one except Grandma Ruby. And don't get me wrong, she did her best and I'm glad I had her, but there's always been something missing, you know?"

Naomi nodded in understanding.

Lucius was surprised at how much he'd shared with her. He usually kept his feelings and thoughts closer to the vest, but with Naomi, he could open up. Be himself.

"I'm sorry, Lucius. It must have been awfully lonely for you."

"It was, but I made do. And eventually I made friends with Adam."

"Your attorney. The one who contacted Kelsey?"

Lucius nodded, chuckling softly. "Adam is my man. There is no one I trust more than him."

"And what about your father?" Naomi inquired. "The article never mentioned him."

Lucius stood up straight. "I don't have one."

"What do you mean? Everyone has a father."

"I don't."

"Then you've missed out," Naomi said, "but you don't have to anymore. You should come with me to Sunday dinner. You could meet my parents and siblings. See what it's like to be part of a real family."

Why the hell had she just invited him to her parents' for dinner? The words were already out of her mouth and Lucius was staring back at her dumbfounded before she could take them back. The invitation was pure impulse, but her reaction to hearing his story wasn't. She felt for the little kid who'd grown up essentially an orphan without either of his parents. Naomi wanted to show him that there was more to life than the hand he'd been dealt.

Of course, the way he was looking at her was giving her serious reservations about the hastiness of her invitation.

Eventually, however, Lucius spoke. "Come to your parents' with *you*?"

Naomi nodded. All of sudden her throat felt parched, and she felt like she was dying of thirst. She always had this reaction around Lucius, especially when he looked at her. Except this time, there was something different than the lust she usually saw—there was something akin to gratitude.

"Thank you, I think I might like that."

"You would?"

A grin spread across his gorgeous, sinful lips. "Yeah, does that surprise you?"

"Actually, yes. Lucius Knight at a family dinner."

He shrugged. "Well, it's as you've said. I've never been a family man."

"Well, perhaps it's time you tried it on for size."

And Lucius was willing to do just that, especially if Naomi was included in the package. The more time he spent with her, the more he knew that she was something special. She was single-handedly starting to renew his faith in human kindness and compassion. Something he'd long since forgotten.

"Well, we've made it to my car," Naomi said several seconds later when they arrived in the nearly deserted parking lot. Lucius rolled down his trousers and put on his shoes. Naomi did the same, pushing down her capris and donning the flats she'd been carrying.

She unlocked her car door with her keyless entry. "Thanks a—"

Naomi never got another syllable out, because Lucius covered the ground between them in a split second and scooped the lower half of her against him and then crashed his mouth down on hers. He'd wanted to kiss her from the moment he'd seen her on the beach, but he'd reined in his desire for her.

But now, before she left, he wanted to taste her. Tilting her head for better access, he plundered her mouth like he'd never done with any other woman. He wanted this to be better than any kiss she'd ever had from another man.

He tantalized and tasted her with gentle strokes of his lips. His tongue glided across hers, exciting them both until she moved her hands to his shoulders. She slid her arms around his neck and held his head to hers. And when he seductively, expertly, slid his tongue between her lips, she responded with provocative probes of her own. The way she was responding to him was wildly exhilarating.

He pressed farther into her, backing her up against the car so she could feel the hard evidence of his arousal. Naomi moaned, ramping up the fierce passion surging through him. Lucius meshed their mouths together, driving for more pleasure.

His heart was pounding loudly in his chest. He was so

damn hot for her. He didn't care that he was damn near sexing her on the street. He just wanted more. He clutched her bottom, grinding her even closer, and that's when he felt her nipples rake against his chest. If he didn't stop himself, she would goad him into losing control. What was she doing to him? She was like a drug that he just had to have a hit of.

It took effort, but Lucius pulled back, breaking their kiss. When he did, they both sucked in air, but he didn't let her go. He liked having Naomi against him. He stared down into her eyes—they were wild and dilated. "I want you, Naomi, but it can't be here. It can't be now."

They were in plain view of anyone walking by, and he was sure they'd already given the odd passerby quite a show.

Slowly, he shifted, loosening his grasp, and opened the driver's side door. He tucked Naomi inside. "But we will be together soon," he whispered. "You can count on it."

"He said, you'll be together soon and that you could count on it?" Kelsey asked as Naomi laid out her mat at her Lamaze class several days later at Long Beach Memorial, where Kelsey would be having her baby.

Naomi had agreed to be a fill-in for Kelsey's husband, Owen, who'd had to leave unexpectedly on a business trip. Naomi had to admit that she was thrilled for some time with her best friend. With their busy schedules and Kelsey working from home, sometimes it was hard to link up.

"Yes," Naomi answered.

"And when was this again?"

"A few days ago," Naomi said, offering Kelsey her hand so she could help her onto the mat, "when we ran into each other on the beach."

"Are you sure that was just a coincidence?" Kelsey inquired, accepting her hand. "I mean, he did follow you to Anaheim for the conference."

"That isn't what happened."

Kelsey's brow rose. "No? First we get an offer from Knight International and then suddenly you run into him at a natural products expo?"

"I suppose you're right, but the beach was different. He was visibly upset and genuinely shocked to see me. He'd just had a run-in with his mother that I gathered didn't go well."

"A man at odds with his family? That isn't good," Kelsey replied.

"It's not like that," Naomi defended Lucius. "His mother has been MIA since he was born and from the little bit I've gathered, he doesn't have a father. You should feel compassion for him."

"I don't need to. You're doing enough of that for the both of us, Naomi. You always did have a soft heart. And I fear that Lucius is playing right into it."

"I disagree. And even if I did, it doesn't matter now, because I invited him to my parents' for dinner."

"You did what?"

The Lamaze instructor clapped her hands. "Class, is everyone ready to begin?"

"I invited him to dinner," Naomi whispered in Kelsey's ear as the class began. "To let him see a real family in action."

An hour later, as Naomi rolled up the mat, Kelsey picked the conversation back up.

"This is a bad idea, Naomi," Kelsey said once she was on her feet, "letting this man into your life. You know little to nothing about him and suddenly he's meeting your parents?"

"Kelsey, I'm not introducing him as my man or anything. Why are you getting so bent out of shape?"

"When was the last time you introduced your parents to the man in your life?"

Naomi rolled her eyes upward. When was the last time? She couldn't remember.

"That's right. Do the math, Naomi. You've never invited a man to meet your family, now suddenly you've invited Lucius Knight? I don't think you're being completely honest with yourself or me. I think you feel more for this man than you're letting on. And I'm just afraid for you, darling. You wear your heart on your sleeve, and Lucius is just the kind of rotten scoundrel to stomp all over it."

Was Kelsey right? Her feelings for Lucius had grown exponentially since seeing him again a couple of weeks ago. And the attraction between with them hadn't cooled. In fact, it had gotten stronger, more potent and more palpable. Sitting at work, all she had to do was think of Lucius or his kisses and her blood pressure would skyrocket. Was she going down a rabbit hole? *Would* Lucius stomp all over her heart?

"So what's going on with your quest to obtain Brooks and Johnson?" Adam asked Lucius when they met up for drinks the next day at a gentleman's club. Lucius had been busy working on another takeover project and hadn't had time to catch up with Adam, though he'd left several messages. "You haven't mentioned it in days. I thought you wanted the company."

"I do." Lucius loosened his tie. After wearing a suit for a long day at the office, he was ready to relax. His jacket was already slung over the back of his chair. "But as you know, Naomi isn't interested in selling."

"But there's always her partner, Kelsey."

"And how has that been coming?"

"Slowly," Adam replied. "I've spoken with her once and since then she's given me the cold shoulder. Said she was too busy to get back to me."

Lucius leaned back in his chair and regarded his friend. "I suspect Naomi is the reason for Kelsey's lack of interest. I'm sure she's pitching to her that selling would not be in the best interest of their company."

Adam reached for his glass of bourbon. "But our offer is more than generous. Kelsey would be a fool to turn it down."

"You haven't met Naomi. I've never met a more stubborn woman in my entire life. She's infuriating and opinionated and tenacious…" He stopped speaking when he noticed that Adam was staring at him strangely. "What?"

Adam shrugged. "Sounds like you're pretty hung up on the woman all of a sudden."

Lucius laughed and attempted to make light of the situation. "No, what I want to do is put her over my knee and spank her." An image of Naomi lying over his thigh with her bottom facing him sprang into his mind. He'd love nothing better than to give that delicious little bottom of hers a spank before he…

"Lucius!"

He blinked. "What?"

Adam shook his head while an amused grin spread across his lips. "You've got it bad, dude."

"For Naomi?" Lucius sipped his scotch neat. "You couldn't be more wrong. What I do have is a little bit of sexual frustration, and once it's released, I'll be right as rain."

"Sure," Adam responded. "If you think that's all it is."

Of course that's all it is, Lucius thought. Despite his sexual attraction toward Naomi, he didn't want or need any romantic complications. Naomi was the type of woman that a man got serious about and married. Lucius was not the marrying kind. And never would be. He needed to focus on his two objectives. One was getting his hands on Brooks and Johnson. The second was getting Naomi in his bed, and the dinner with her family was his ticket in.

Chapter 8

Naomi was nervous as she waited for Lucius to come pick her up at her home in Belmont Heights. Why hadn't she asked him to meet her at her parents' instead of picking her up? Now he not only would know where she lived—though he probably already had a file on her—but this was starting to look a lot like a date. She hadn't had one of those in God knew how long. Brooks and Johnson's rapid growth had caused Naomi to put her love life on the shelf.

She'd focused on building her brand rather than making any lasting connections with men. And it had cost her. At thirty-two, she'd only had one or two serious relationships, and dating had been nonexistent the last couple of years. She'd envied Kelsey. Her friend had always made time for romance and subsequently had met and fallen in love with her husband, Owen, five years ago. Now Naomi was all alone and forced to face the dating scene solo. And since she'd always been awkward around men, the thought of going out clubbing or online dating hadn't appealed to her. Which would explain why she was so nervous. She was about to spend the evening with Lucius Knight. He was not only her high school crush and the first boy she'd ever wanted, but he also happened to be one of the sexiest men alive, in her opinion.

She knew she shouldn't, but Naomi couldn't help herself and dressed with Lucius in mind. She wanted him to see her as desirable. She'd taken care by spiral rodding her natural curls so they now hung in ringlets to her shoulders. And she'd dressed in a fuchsia maxi skirt with a button-down denim shirt and extra-wide belt that showed off her curves. Naomi fully expected Lucius to be shocked when he saw her.

She was right.

Lucius stared at Naomi when she opened the door to her home. He hadn't known exactly what the appropriate attire for an evening with her family would be and hoped that his casual approach of dark jeans, plaid shirt and cable-knit V-neck sweater was the right look. He'd been right, because she was wearing a high-waisted maxi skirt that showed off her amazing slender waist and hugged her hips. He liked that the denim shirt was open just enough to allow her gold necklace to dangle between her breasts and show him a slight swell of cleavage.

Lucius swallowed. How was he supposed to keep his hands to himself when she dressed like that?

"I'm ready," Naomi stated with her hobo bag over her shoulder and a light jacket in her hand. Before he could take a step inside her home, she closed the door behind her.

He smiled. If that was how she wanted to play it, that was fine, but Lucius knew that before the night was over, he would be coming inside, and not just in her home.

"Great, let's go." He gently placed his hand at the small of her back and led her to his Bentley parked outside on the curb, but not before whispering in her ear, "By the way, you look gorgeous."

She glanced up at him. "Thank you."

After helping her inside, he came around to the driver's side and hopped in. "You lead the way," he said as he started the engine.

They chatted easily on the twenty-minute ride to her parents' home. Naomi told him about their history. "You'll love them. They've been married for thirty-five years and are as still in love as they were when they first met."

"That's pretty amazing considering the divorce rate," Lucius responded.

"I know, right?" Naomi gave him a sideways glance. "Trust me, I know how lucky I am to have my parents together after all these years."

"And you have a brother, Tim, and sister, Gemma, right?"

She smiled when she looked at him again. "You remembered."

"I do listen," Lucius said, "it's a must in business."

"And is that what tonight is?" Naomi asked, a frown quickly spreading across her mouth. "Because I didn't ask you here on business. I asked you as a friend."

"Duly noted," Lucius replied. "And I am here as your *friend*." He emphasized the word even though he didn't want to be her friend. He wanted to be her lover. "I've put business on the shelf tonight."

"Glad to hear it."

They parked in front of her father's Mercedes-Benz several minutes later and exited the vehicle. Lucius grabbed the rare bottle of wine he'd obtained from the gourmet store for dinner along with a bouquet of calla lilies for Naomi's mother.

"You didn't have to do that," Naomi said when he met her at the front door just as she was opening it.

"I know, but my grandma Ruby did raise me with some manners," he answered with a smile.

"Naomi!" A beautiful petite woman with a caramel complexion and dressed in a wraparound print dress met them in foyer. She had Naomi's exact same riotous curls.

"Mom!"

Lucius watched Naomi bend down to lean into her mother's embrace and felt his heart constrict. He and Jocelyn never hugged. They barely touched.

"And you must be Lucius," her mother said, and before he could answer she enveloped him in a warm, motherly hug. Surprise must have been evident on his face, because he noticed Naomi mouth *it's okay*, so he hugged her back.

"Thank you for having me, ma'am," Lucius responded when they parted. "I brought you some flowers and wine." He presented her with the bouquet and bottle of rare wine.

Mrs. Brooks beamed with pleasure. "You shouldn't have, but thank you. They're lovely. Come on inside." She slid her arm through his and led him into the home. "So you can meet the rest of the family."

Five minutes later, Lucius had been introduced to the entire Brooks family. Her father, Benjamin, was a big bear of a man with a grip to match. Her brother, Tim, who although not as muscular as his father was just as tall as Lucius, eyed him suspiciously. Tim's wife, Audrey, was a quiet, unassuming woman who suited him to perfection. And they had a precocious four-year-old daughter, Grace, who wanted to be the center of attention. Then there was Naomi's sister, Gemma. She was sassy and just as fiery as Naomi, if not more. She wasted no time firing questions at him. He liked them all immediately.

"So, Lucius," Gemma asked when they all sat in the living room, "do you remember going to high school with my sister?"

Lucius sat beside Naomi on the love seat while her father sat in a recliner, her mother stood passing around appetizers and refreshments before dinner, while her brother and his wife sat opposite them on the sofa.

He felt Naomi tense at her sister's question, but he patted her knee lightly. "Actually, I do," he said with a smile. "I remember Naomi was a bit shy."

"Shy?" Gemma laughed out loud. "She was more like a nerd!"

"Gemma!" Her mother wagged her finger at her. "That's not nice."

"Sorry, Mom." Gemma acted like she was remorseful, but Lucius highly doubted it. As the youngest, he suspected Gemma was used to being coddled instead of being given the discipline she so desperately needed. The Brooks family wasn't perfect, but that's what made them real. "But you know it's true," she continued. "Back then, all Naomi did was have her head in a book."

"Unlike you?" Naomi responded. "Who was always into cheerleading and boys."

"Hey, don't hate me because I was popular," Gemma replied with a smirk.

"And were you popular, too?" Her brother directed a question to Lucius.

"Not at all." Lucius slid his arm along the back of the love seat behind Naomi. It was a casual move, but told Tim man-to-man that his interest in his sister was of a romantic nature. He saw Naomi's eyes widen, but she didn't say anything.

"Afraid not," he finally answered. "Like Naomi, I was more of an outcast."

"A bad boy, if the papers tell it correctly," Timothy responded.

Lucius shrugged. "Bad boy, outcast. Does it really matter now?"

"Not at all," Mr. Brooks stated from his recliner, "only matters what a man makes of himself when the dust settles. And from the looks of it, you haven't done too bad for yourself, Lucius."

"No, sir. I've done quite well."

"Dinner is ready," Mrs. Brooks said when she reentered the room. Lucius hadn't even seen her leave. He'd been so engrossed in the family dynamics. Was this what it was like being part of a family? If so, he could get used to this.

Naomi smiled as she watched Lucius interact with her family. He was a natural and fit right in. He was charming to her mother. Forthright to her father. And accommodating to Tim, who pulled no punches in his direct questioning of Lucius.

Her brother had drilled Lucius, wanting to know how he'd gotten his start, when he created Knight International and more. Naomi was just glad that Tim had heeded her earlier call when she'd begged him not to bring business or Lucius's interest in Brooks and Johnson into the conversation. Her father also wasn't stopping. He made sure to question Lucius about his background. That's when she felt Lucius's mood change.

"So tell us about your family?" her father asked. "Your mother and father, what do they do?"

"Dad," Naomi interjected. "You remember I told you that Lucius was raised by his grandmother." She glanced to her side and saw the firm set of Lucius's jaw.

"Oh, of course, I'm sorry, son," her father replied. "I didn't mean anything by it."

"No offense taken," Lucius responded. "My background

is no secret. My father wasn't around, and my mother chose not to raise me. Lucky for me, my grandma stepped in."

Naomi noticed he plastered a fake smile on, but she knew otherwise. This topic of conversation made Lucius uneasy.

"Do you even know your father?" Gemma asked from the other end of the table.

Naomi choked on the water she'd been sipping and her brother had to pat her on the back. She shot Gemma a cold look as she wiped her mouth and watched Lucius warily. His eyes were impenetrable and she couldn't fathom what was going on in his mind.

"No, I do not." He was to the point and it was stated with such finality that even Gemma busied herself with refilling her wineglass.

"Well, how about some dessert?" her mother asked.

Bless her heart. Naomi couldn't have been more thankful for the distraction and change of the conversation. The set of Lucius's mouth was grim, and the smile that had been on his face throughout the course of the evening had faded. In its place was a sullen and withdrawn man. A man who reminded her of the teenage boy she'd once fallen for.

Dessert continued with Naomi and her mother doing their best to revive the conversation. Lucius made polite chitchat and was never rude in any way, but Naomi could tell that the earlier conversation had rattled him.

After the meal, she and Lucius said their goodbyes as her family walked them to the door. Her father shook Lucius's hand while her mother once again enveloped him in a hug. As he bent down to accept it, Naomi could see Lucius warm up slightly at the contact.

"Thank you both for having me over," Lucius said once they'd parted. "I truly appreciate the hospitality."

"You're welcome any time, son," her father said, placing

his arm around her mother. Then he turned to Naomi. "So feel free to bring this young man around again."

Naomi smiled. Then she stood on her tiptoes to give her father a kiss on the cheek. "Thanks, Daddy."

Lucius opened the front door and once again placed his hand on the small of her back and led her outside.

Naomi shivered slightly. The air had turned crisp. Lucius wrapped his arm around her as he walked her to the car. Once inside, she glanced up and saw her parents peeking at them through the curtains. She smiled and shook her head as Lucius hopped inside.

They were quiet on the drive back to Belmont Heights. She knew he didn't like talking about himself and family was a sore spot for him, but she wished she knew more and why he was closed up about that side of himself. Transparency was not his strong suit. Whereas she wore her heart on her sleeve.

When they made it to her house and he turned off the engine, Naomi turned to him. "Did you have fun tonight?"

Lucius slid around to face her in his seat. "I did. You have a really great family."

Naomi stared at him questioningly. "Are you sure about that?"

His brow furrowed. "Why would you ask that?"

"Because… I think you were having a good time until my sister asked you about your father. After that, well, let's just say you were a cold fish."

He grinned. "A cold fish?"

"Yes, and don't go grinning like that," Naomi said, pointing her finger at him, "and trying to be all charming now. Where was this guy an hour ago? I want to know where he went and why."

"If you let me inside, perhaps I'll tell you why," he countered. His steady gaze bored into her.

There was a maddening arrogance to him that drove Naomi crazy. She hated that when he looked at her she was powerless to resist him. If she let him in, Naomi knew what it meant, and it caused her heart to jolt and her pulse to pound. There was no denying that alone in her house with no distractions, no interruptions, she would give in to her attraction to Lucius. She'd been trying to fight it for weeks. What would happen if she unlocked her heart, her soul, her body to this man? Should she chance it? She'd always wanted this man, wanted to know what it would be like to be with him. What was wrong with allowing herself this one night of pleasure with her heart's desire?

She knew her answer and spoke quickly before she changed her mind. "Come inside."

Lucius felt triumphant when he walked through the doors of Naomi's home. It had been no easy feat getting Naomi to let go, but she finally had. However, there was a catch. He would have to open up and bare part of his soul to her in exchange.

He rarely spoke of his feelings about his family or lack thereof to anyone. What he'd told her before was more than he'd told any of his former companions—and yet she still wanted more and he would give it to her. What did that mean? Was she becoming more to him than just a means to an end?

He looked up from the sofa where he'd made himself comfortable while Naomi busied herself in the kitchen with refreshments. Did she need liquid courage to be with him? Or was it for him so he would feel more comfortable talking about his past?

He liked Naomi's house. It was warm and inviting, like the woman herself. He liked the outside with the covered front porch, travertine stone walkways, landscaped planters and mature palm trees. The inside was just as appealing as the exterior, with hardwood and ceramic tile floors in the front of the house. The living room had a built-in wet bar and etched French doors that led to a large balcony, which he was sure had gorgeous sunset views.

He turned around when he heard footsteps. Naomi returned with a tray holding a bottle of cabernet sauvignon, two wineglasses and an opener. She set the tray down on the unusual cocktail table that was made of treated wood and sat on the sofa.

"Would you mind uncorking?" She handed him the wine opener.

"Not at all." He uncorked the bottle and poured them both glasses. He handed her one and held up his glass. "To new beginnings."

"Is that what this is?" Naomi asked. Her eyes were unreadable.

"I hope so." He placed his glass on the table and turned to face her. "You asked me in, so it's a start."

She leaned back against the sofa cushions. "I did. So why don't we start with why you got so standoffish after my sister's inquiry."

So they were jumping right into the deep end? No preamble. He sighed. "All right, I suppose I was a little guarded."

"Yes, why is that, Lucius?" She sipped her wine. "The other day you mentioned your relationship with your mother isn't good."

There was no judgment in her eyes, just questions. So he answered honestly. "Because it's a sore subject for me. Family, that is. I don't like talking about my lack of one."

"Because you don't know your father?" Naomi pressed, "Lots of kids today are growing up without their father around."

Lucius chuckled. "So are you telling me to get over myself?

"Not at all, I'm just saying that fatherless black children are no longer the exception, but the rule. While I'm the exception, having both my parents together."

"Your family is truly exceptional," Lucius stated. "I really enjoyed them tonight."

"Thank you, but don't try to deflect the conversation. You're not getting off that easy."

He smirked. "I didn't think I would. The thing is, Naomi, I'm angry. I'm angry because I've been denied the right to know my father."

Naomi blinked with bafflement. "I don't understand."

"When I say I don't know my father, I'm not saying I don't have a relationship with him," Lucius replied. "I mean I don't know *who* he is. My mother refuses to tell me."

"Has she told you why?"

He shook his head. "Not in so many words, but I suspect that he's married."

"That's awful."

"And no matter how much I beg and plead, it falls on deaf ears. She won't give up his identity. Last week, when you found me on the beach, I'd just come from seeing her. You see, she comes for a visit every now and then to ease her conscience that she isn't a terrible person and mother. And every time I ask her who my father is, she denies me."

He could see tears well in Naomi's eyes and knew she felt sorry for him. Lucius hated pity, but since he was going into the deep end of the ocean, he might as well go all in. "All my life, I've looked in the crowd, wondering if that man or that man—" he pointed in the air "—could be my father. You have no idea how demoralizing it is. I know I'm someone's bastard, but whose?"

Naomi quickly rose, set her wineglass on the cocktail table and scooted closer to him. "Don't say that, Lucius." She grabbed his chin in one hand. "You're nobody's bastard."

When she let him go, he continued, "I know that here—" he pointed to his head "—but not here." He pointed to his chest. "Why shouldn't I feel this way?" He could feel tears biting the backs of his eyes, but he never cried. "So if I'm guarded or have walls up when it comes to this subject, that's why. And tonight, seeing your family and how much you guys love each other and show affection, it—it touched me." His voice broke as he placed his hand over his heart.

Naomi reached for him then, pulling him into her arms. She squeezed him hard, letting him know that it was all right to feel the emotions he was feeling. Lucius didn't realize just how much he'd needed to say the words and let out emotions he'd carried inside for years, to share his burden with someone else. What was it about Naomi that caused him to be so open? Was it that he'd finally found someone with depth, something he'd avoided his entire life?

Lucius didn't know why. All he knew was that her hug felt good, and he held on tighter, breathing in her feminine scent. He buried his head in her neck and inhaled deeply. She smelled so good, so sweet. He liked having her against him, feeling her nipples against his chest. If someone asked him later when her embrace turned from comfort to something else, he couldn't tell them, but it did. He pulled away from Naomi and his eyes raked her boldly seconds before they reached for each other and began kissing passionately.

Chapter 9

Naomi had to have this man. She'd imagined this moment in her teenage fantasies but never thought it would actually come true, but even her dreams were not as perfect as this moment. She swayed in his arms and they fell backward onto the couch. She knew how wrong this could turn out for her. What if he was just interested in her business and not her? The way he kissed her told her he felt *something* for her, even if it was just lust. A wild tingling formed in her breasts and her nipples had turned to bullets.

When he pulled away and rose from the couch, Naomi thought he might be having second thoughts, but instead, he scooped her up in his arms and started down the hall. "Bedroom?"

"Door on the left," Naomi murmured as Lucius's lips swept over hers again.

When she glanced up, she was in her room and Lucius was laying her down on her king-size bed. She'd always loved how large and sumptuous it was, and now she would have someone to share it with.

She watched Lucius toe off his shoes and shed his cable-knit sweater and plaid shirt until he was standing in front of her in dark jeans slung low on his hips. Naomi drank him in. He was sexy as hell and had a physique to go with it. His chest was broad and hairless, letting her know he kept up with his manscaping. His pectorals and abs were equally impressive. She couldn't wait to see what the rest of him looked like.

Lucius was so male that it stirred every female sensation within her. She could feel her toes curl in anticipation of what was to come. With openmouthed awe, she watched him unzip and remove his jeans until he was in nothing but his boxer briefs. His erection was straining against the fabric, and her mouth watered.

He stepped forward and joined her on the bed, his weight lowering the mattress. "Did you like what you saw?"

Naomi smiled. "I loved every minute of the striptease."

"Good," Lucius murmured huskily. "Because it's your turn."

Naomi's heart fluttered in her chest. She knew she had a nice body, but she wasn't used to being on display. She tried to sit up, but Lucius lightly pushed backward.

"Oh, no." He wagged his finger. "I intend to unwrap this gift, one delicious moment at a time, but first..."

She could think of nothing else because Lucius's mouth covered hers and demanded a response. His tongue dived inside her mouth, swirling around hers in a delicious duel that Naomi wanted to lose. Feeling his warm skin against hers made her suck on his tongue voraciously, devouring him as his hands roamed up and down her body. His muscles were so hard and it fascinated her, she couldn't wait to explore him with her fingers, but Lucius was in control.

There wasn't an inch of her he didn't touch. His hands outlined the swell of her breasts, her hips and the curve of her bottom. He pulled her closer into his manhood, and

Naomi moaned. She wanted him desperately, more than she'd ever wanted another man. As if sensing her urgency, he unbuckled her wide belt and tossed it aside. Then his hands were at the waist of her maxi skirt, sliding it down her hips ever so slowly. He stopped kissing her long enough to ease the skirt off and let it fall to the floor.

He looked down at her, his hard, muscular forearms on either side of her. "I can't wait to see more of you." He reached for the buttons of her denim shirt, and Naomi felt cool air as Lucius opened the shirt to his openly admiring gaze. His fingers played with the latch of her front-closure bra until the snap unlocked and her breasts spilled out.

Lucius's eyes darkened. "You're beautiful," he said. "I have to taste you." He lowered his head and feasted on her brown globes and chocolate nipples. He took one nipple in his mouth and rolled his tongue across the sensitive tip. Naomi squirmed underneath him. Heat whooshed at the apex of her thighs as if driven by some primal instinct of being with this man.

She cupped the back of his head as he continued nibbling gently. She didn't want him to stop. And she needn't have worried, because he kept his attention on the task at hand, which was sampling her other breast. Lucius seemed intent on exploring every inch of her body with leisurely strokes of his tongue. All she had to do was lie back and enjoy it.

Naomi Brooks was a feast for any man, Lucius thought. Soft curves, ample breasts, long legs and a flat stomach. She was every man's fantasy, and he couldn't wait to take her, but he would do so slowly, reverently, because he'd waited long enough to have this woman. Taking a woman to bed usually came easily for him, but Naomi was different. She'd made him work for the privilege of being with her, and he respected her for it, which made him want her all the more.

Lucius lifted his head and looked into her passion-glazed brown eyes. Naomi was expressive and showed him she enjoyed everything he was doing.

"I-is something wrong?" she asked softly.

"Not at all. I'm just enjoying the view." Lucius's hand roamed from her breasts down her rib cage to her stomach and lower to her panties. He hooked his hand around the band and slid them down her thighs until she was completely naked. She wasn't embarrassed—not when he stared at her with open admiration. Lucius allowed himself to stroke her hips, then her thighs, until he came to the heat of her. He rested his hand there for a moment and felt Naomi tremble beneath his touch. How much more would she when his tongue and fingers were buried inside her?

He had to find out.

His thumb caressed her softly, playing with the soft folds of her womanhood. He licked his lips when he found she was wet for him. He lowered his head to lick and suck on her breast whilst he slid one long finger inside her. She was hot and tight. Damn.

"Oh!" she cried out.

His body thickened, tightening in painful response, but he had to wait. He wanted her ready for him. He tormented her with his hand as his mouth swept a trail of hot kisses down her abdomen to arrow in on the dark springy curls at the entrance to the intimate part of her. He could smell her womanly scent. It was heady for any man, and he was no different. He dipped his tongue into the soft folds of her sex, intent on driving Naomi to a fever pitch. He exulted in tasting all of her sweet wetness. He grasped her bottom so he could stroke her over and over with his tongue.

Naomi's moans were letting him know that tension was

building up inside her. She clutched at his shoulders and tried to tug his body over hers, but he didn't oblige, not yet. He wanted to send her over the edge and only then would he join her on the ride. His tongue darted farther inside her until he reached to the hilt, and Naomi screamed.

"Lucius!" Her hips bucked and her back arched off the bed.

He licked all her slick juices as her orgasm hit her full force. When he lifted his head, he saw the glaze in her eyes and smiled. He slid off the bed long enough to find the condom packets he'd thrown in his pocket. He'd been sure that tonight was the night he'd make Naomi his, and he'd been right.

As he rejoined her on the bed after protecting them, she whispered, "I need you inside me."

"I'm happy to oblige," Lucius said, using his weight to push her legs apart. He'd been aching for her and now he would find out just how good she felt. Lucius surged into her slick passage. The fusion of their two bodies together caused a torrent of sensations to explode through him. He wasn't prepared for it, and being with her would cause him to lose every vestige of control.

Naomi reached for Lucius, circling her arms around his neck, and he dropped his head so he could ravish her with his mouth. She'd just had a soul-shattering climax that had ripped through her body, but there was more waiting. She wanted all of Lucius and locked her legs around him, taking him deeper to the very edge of her. She clamped around him and moaned at the intense satisfaction of having Lucius buried inside her. Her hands slid up and down his back clamoring for the sensations that were electrifying her each time Lucius thrust into her.

Both were eager and impatient to go over the edge to

complete and utter satiation. They moved together in unison, rocking their hips. A storm was brewing and they rode it, hurtling over and over at a breakneck speed as if their very lives hung in the balance of this one moment. Lucius quickened his pace, and Naomi could feel her body tighten, her inner muscles flex. And when he thrust inside her one last time, they both reached the peak and shattered violently, sending them both flying over the precipice.

Naomi's arms dropped from his shoulders and flopped onto the mattress. She was amazed. Sex had never been this good. She'd never known it could be this way, but Lucius had brought out something in her she hadn't known existed. No matter what happened between them, she would always be grateful for that. She was a sexual woman and now she knew it.

"Look who's grinning like a Cheshire cat," Lucius commented as he propped on one elbow and looked down at her. He wondered what she was thinking, feeling. It appeared she was happily satisfied with tonight's outcome and that she didn't regret her decision to be with him.

Her mouth quirked. "I'm not the only one. You seem pretty smug yourself."

He grinned. "Mmm…that was very good." Their lovemaking had been a fantastic journey—her response to him and how it made him feel had been a cataclysmic moment. They'd both free-fallen on a sweet cloud of ecstasy. And now they were in a relaxed embrace, with his other arm holding her against him.

He usually wasn't the cuddling type, but he was tonight. Maybe it was the sweet scent of her skin or her wispy damp curls that he twirled between his fingers or the rise and fall of her breasts. Whatever it was, he liked it and he didn't want to leave. Plus, he hadn't nearly had his fill of

Naomi. He'd been driven by a need to take Naomi, to possess her. And he had. He couldn't explain the animal instinct that had taken over him, but the chemistry between them went deep. He wouldn't be satisfied until he'd fully explored it and Naomi.

The next morning, Naomi was exhausted, but satiated because she'd been woken up twice by Lucius during the night to slow, erotic caresses, which instantly stimulated her all over. The first time together had been epic because they'd been frenzied, wanting to rip each other's clothes off and come together. In the wee hours of the morning, he'd lingered, touching every curve, making Naomi exultant in her womanliness. Then they'd both begun an exploration of each other's bodies.

She now knew every intimate detail of his muscled frame. Had even aroused him when she'd taken his shaft between her palms and heard his sharp intake of breath. She'd experimented, stroking him with light touches, then with flicks of her tongue over steel until she'd taken him into her mouth. He'd moaned her name, clutching the back of her head to help her take him even deeper. She'd loved giving him head and how it had made her feel skilled that she could arouse a man like Lucius.

He was an expert lover, and each time was more marvelous than the last. Naomi hadn't been prepared for how incredibly exciting it was to be free of her inhibitions sexually. With Lucius, she'd discovered a world of endless possibilities and heightened pleasures she hadn't known existed.

When she finally rolled over to look at him, he was still asleep. His brilliant dark eyes were closed, but his face was just as strong and handsome as ever. Naomi sighed all over again at how absolutely gorgeous this man was. He had the right amount of muscles to his well-proportioned body and loads of sex appeal. She didn't have any regrets over the amazing night she'd spent with him.

Careful not to wake him, she slid out of bed.

Lucius stretched his arms leisurely as he awoke. He hadn't expected Naomi to be all liquid heat and trembling passion in his arms, but she had been. She'd been bold and daring with him, he suspected more than she'd ever been with her previous lovers.

He'd delayed his own satisfaction several times during the night to ensure that she was completely satisfied.

"Coffee?"

Lucius blinked into focus and saw Naomi dressed in a robe and standing beside her bed—holding out an unstylish mug that looked like she'd made it. Obviously it was for him, so he sat up, pushing the pillows against the headboard, and accepted the proffered mug. "Thank you." He took a sip of the coffee. "You're up early."

"Couldn't sleep."

"That means I didn't do my job and tire you out," he said with a gleam of amusement. "Perhaps I need to try again." He placed his mug on the nightstand beside him, and before Naomi could say no, pulled her back onto the bed and into his lap.

"Lucius…" Her shock at his manhandling caused her mouth to gape open, and his tongue immediately slid inside. He kissed her slowly, confidently until he felt her sweet sigh of surrender.

He pulled at the belt that held her robe closed until it loosened and he could feast his eyes on her breasts. He reached for them, the fullness just enough for his palm, as if they were made for him and only him. Her nipples grew into buds at his touch. He liked that he had that effect on her.

He bent his head and suckled languorously on each nipple, circling the engorged tips with his tongue until they were stiff and wet. He glanced up at her and saw that her eyes were shut tight, so he licked his way down her body. He couldn't wait to come to her sex and once again make Naomi his.

"Inside me," Naomi pleaded when she felt Lucius tongue swirling into her navel. She appreciated all the foreplay. Lucius was a master at it, but she wanted him inside her.

"Shh," he soothed, reaching up to press his palm against the lower part of her stomach. "Relax, I promise to give you everything you want and more."

Didn't he know how impossible it was to be still when he was doing all kinds of wicked things to her? His tongue had found its way to her exposed sex and was now circling her core, and then she felt his fingers.

"Lucius," Naomi moaned in pleasure. He was playing her like an instrument, and it was like her body knew every melody. It was responding to him, and the sensations were exhilarating, just like being on a roller coaster ride. Her belly tightened, and her thighs quivered.

He slid away from her body until her back was flat against the mattress. Then he flipped her onto her stomach. She heard the rustle of the foil unwrapping, and then his large palm splayed across her stomach, bringing her bottom into direct contact with his thick erection. Lucius's body curved around hers as he kissed and nibbled on her neck. It was incredibly erotic and even more so when his fingers found their way inside her and began stroking her again.

Naomi sucked in a deep breath. Mercy. The man had a way with his hands.

Lucius scooped her up to place her on her knees, his hands grasped her hips and he surged into her. Holding her firmly, he began to rock back and forth, slowly at first, withdrawing slightly so as to not hurt her, brushing her curls aside so he could kiss the back of her neck. Then he would thrust in again until he was buried deep.

She could hear his heavy breathing as he pounded into her, feel his thrusts coming faster and faster. Naomi clutched at her duvet as sensation after sensation assaulted her. Pressure was building up inside her, tighter and tighter, threatening to break. She clenched her inner walls to hold him snug inside her, but it didn't work. The dam burst, and her entire body spasmed as wave after wave of pleasure engulfed her.

Lucius roared behind her and lifted her off the bed, clutching her body to him as his orgasm struck. Then they both fell forward, glued to each other in a mass of limbs. Eventually, he rolled off her and onto his back, but Naomi was spent and could only lie there with her hot face pressed against the cool pillow.

A delicious feeling of peace came over her. She was finding every aspect of this scenario and each orgasm he gave her extremely satisfying. How in the world would she ever get tired of making love to this man? But she would have to, because Lucius Knight was a no-commitment kind of guy.

Chapter 10

Naomi couldn't think, much less concentrate on anything but the torrent of sensations still assailing her body after spending yet another night with Lucius. She hadn't intended on becoming intimate with Lucius when she'd invited him to dinner at her parents' nearly two weeks ago. She'd wanted to show him what a normal family looked like. She'd had no idea how Gemma bringing up Lucius's parentage would send their relationship down a different course.

She hadn't known what to expect after spending the night with Lucius, didn't have much in the way of experience with casual relationships. She most certainly wasn't prepared that she'd see him every evening afterward, but she had. And it had been sheer and utter bliss ever since.

Lucius called her every day at work or texted her just to say hi. Or he would ask her to dinner, taking her to fine dining establishments that, although she could now afford them, she had never frequented. One Friday after work, he'd called her and told her to put on her sexiest outfit because he was taking her out dancing. She'd done as he'd asked and was happy to discover that Lucius was just as good at dancing as he was at every other task he put his mind to. His moves were smooth and assured on the dance floor, and he handled her with ease.

Naomi recalled a particularly sensual moment when he'd slid his leg between hers and gyrated his hips against hers. She blushed at the memory of the heated sensations that had flooded her body and the way he'd made love to her later that night until she begged him to ease the ache between her thighs.

Other times, they spent the night at her home, cooking dinner or ordering in and vegging out on her sofa. She was exposing him to life like a regular joe and he was onboard. To her astonishment, they enjoyed the same compelling television shows, like *The Walking Dead* and *Game of Thrones*, and laughed at badly made reality television shows.

"Are you sure you don't want to go out?" Naomi asked one evening after a week of domestication.

Lucius shook his head. "I'm enjoying this. It's a sense of normalcy I've never had before."

The last two weeks with Lucius had been nothing short of pure perfection, especially because he was an amazing lover who knew how to please her. At times fast and furious and other times soft and tender, Lucius knew how to draw out every delicious moment of their time together.

The man had put some kind of spell on her. But hadn't she always somehow known that it would be that way with him? That only *he* could unlock her sexuality unlike any other man?

Instead of going to lunch, Lucius chose to run on the treadmill at his office gym. He was hoping he would figure out what was going on with him. He'd been with Naomi nearly every night the last two weeks since the first night they'd made love except the one night when he'd had to work late. He'd thought he would be able to move on once he'd sampled Naomi's sweetness, but instead he found himself wondering what she was up to and if she was having a good day. More than that, he *wanted* to spend time with her, no matter if they were dining out, dancing or just spending time at home.

He'd never been this comfortable with a woman, so much so that he'd actually done household chores. He'd been positively baffled when she'd asked him to help her change the linen one morning.

"Lucius, do you even know how to make a bed?" she'd asked.

He'd stared at her, a vision in his white dress shirt that barely reached her thighs.

"Why should I have to?" he'd inquired. "I have a maid service."

"Didn't your grandma ever teach you?" she'd asked, stuffing a large down pillow into a pillowcase.

He'd smiled broadly. "Grandma spoiled me. I didn't have much in the way of chores except maybe taking out the trash and mowing the lawn."

"Lucky you." She bent over to tuck the fitted sheet under the mattress. "But you need to learn."

His eyes had traveled to where the shirt she wore was steadily rising up the back of her thighs. He'd abandoned all thought of making the bed and instead walked toward her and spun her around. The shirt had flown upward to her chin, revealing her bare breasts to his hungry gaze.

"Lucius—" Naomi pushed her shirt down "—what are you doing?"

"Having my way with you," he'd said and lowered his lips to hers. She'd responded to him as she always did— with complete abandon, giving her mouth over so his greedy tongue could invade it. His hands had traveled to the shirt, unbuttoning it until her breasts were free, then he'd left her mouth so he could lave one chocolate bud with the tip of his tongue. He wanted to tease her. Play with her.

Anticipation was half the fun and would only increase their appetite. And it had that night. He'd satisfied a hunger until they'd both lain spent and sweaty on the damp linen.

Lucius groaned and began running faster.

He was losing his mind over this woman. Just this morning, they'd left for work together, showing true domesticity like a normal couple. He'd never spent this much time with another woman, but Naomi tempted him to be a different man when he was with her. The weeks he'd just spent with her were pleasure filled and he couldn't believe he actually wanted more of it.

He had to be in some sort of alternate reality or universe because this wasn't him. He didn't do relationships or commitments of any kind. Women were usually invited into his circle for a limited run, but Naomi was quickly becoming a standing engagement. And one he couldn't wait to revisit every night. What did it mean?

Lucius was bewildered. Even more so, because time was winding down. Kelsey Johnson would be having her baby in a couple of months. What would that mean for him and Naomi?

Later that afternoon, Naomi put her growing feelings for Lucius aside for the meeting she had with a bank she hoped would lend her the money to buy out Kelsey's half of their shares. She'd dressed appropriately for the occasion in a business suit and pumps but was nervous as she sat across from the bank executive.

She was less so when she heard his news.

"I'm sorry, Ms. Brooks, but I'll have to turn down your

request for a loan of this size," the bank executive told her as they sat across from each other.

Naomi had been hoping against hope that given the large amount of business Brooks and Johnson was doing at their bank, they would consider loaning her the necessary funds.

"Are you absolutely certain?"

"You don't have much collateral other than your own shares in Brooks and Johnson to leverage," the balding man replied.

"But the company has gone public and I'm quite wealthy," Naomi responded. "I'll have more than enough funds to pay you back."

"True," he stated, "since the IPO, Brooks and Johnson is financially sound and flush with cash, but that could all change in a heartbeat with a down market. It's a huge risk for us. And what about you, Ms. Brooks? If you're unable to pay back the loan, you could potentially lose all your shares in the company you built. Is it really worth it?"

Naomi pondered that very question on her drive back into the office. The bank executive had a point. Was she ready to risk all her shares if B and J's success lulled or they had a bad year? She didn't know; she couldn't predict the future. But what did she do now?

As if he sensed she was thinking of him, her smartphone rang and the display indicated it was Lucius.

Naomi's heart began to flutter. Even knowing they were at odds in business, they were still very much connected physically. Her body had literally ached for his all day.

"Lucius."

"Hey, beautiful," Lucius said on the other end. "How was your day?"

Naomi thought back to her conversation with the

banker. "Not as productive as I'd hoped. No, let me correct that—it was downright disappointing."

"Is there anything I can do?"

She chuckled to herself. *Stop going after my company?* "No."

"Are you sure about that?" he asked huskily. "I have my ways."

"Then perhaps you should come over and show me."

Lucius stared down at the phone in his hand and a large grin spread across his lips. Had Naomi just propositioned him? Yes! And he was more than ready to oblige her. He'd been unable to get Naomi off his mind all day. When he should have been focusing on figures for his next acquisition, his mind wandered to how her hair looked spread out over her pillow. Or the way her eyes dilated when she came.

He licked his lips. He was getting hard just thinking about it. "When should I be over?"

"By seven p.m. And bring dinner."

"I'll see you then," Lucius said. They wouldn't need dessert, because Naomi was a dessert he intended to sample all night long.

Once he'd ended the call, he tried to return to work, but his mind was shot. He could only think of Naomi. She was consuming his thoughts. He'd been useless most of the day. He would much rather have stayed in bed with her all day until he quenched the hunger he had for this woman.

He couldn't understand the hold she had on him, but she did, and if he wasn't careful, he might lose his head. And for Lucius Knight, that simply would never do. He always knew exactly where he was going in his previous relationships and what he wanted, but not with Naomi. With her,

FREE Merchandise and a Cash Reward† are 'in the Cards' for you!

Dear Reader,

We're giving away FREE MERCHANDISE and a CASH REWARD!

Seriously, we'd like to reward you for reading this novel by giving you **FREE MERCHANDISE** worth over $20 retail plus a CASH REWARD! And no purchase is necessary!

You see the Jack of Hearts sticker above? Paste that sticker in the box on the Free Merchandise Voucher inside. Return the Voucher today… and we'll send you Free Merchandise plus a Cash Reward!

Thanks again for reading one of our novels—and enjoy your Free Merchandise and Cash Reward with our compliments!

Pam Powers

Pam Powers

P.S. Look inside to see what Free Merchandise is **"in the cards"** for you!

We'd like to send you two free books like the one you are enjoying now. Your two books have a combined price of over $10 retail, but they are yours to keep absolutely FREE! We'll even send you 2 wonderful surprise gifts and a Cash Reward†. You can't lose!

REMEMBER: Your Free Merchandise, consisting of **2 Free Books** and **2 Free Gifts**, is worth over $20 retail! Plus we'll send you a **Cash Reward** (it's a dollar) which is really the icing on the cake because it's in addition to your FREE Merchandise! No purchase is necessary, so please send for your Free Merchandise today.

Get TWO FREE GIFTS!

We'll also send you 2 wonderful FREE GIFTS (worth about $10 retail), in addition to your 2 Free books and Cash Reward!

Visit us at:
www.ReaderService.com

Books received may not be as shown.

YOUR FREE MERCHANDISE INCLUDES...
2 FREE Books **AND** 2 FREE Mystery Gifts
PLUS you'll get a Cash Reward†

FREE MERCHANDISE VOUCHER

**2 FREE
BOOKS**
and
**2 FREE
GIFTS**

Please send my Free Merchandise, consisting of
2 Free Books and **2 Free Mystery Gifts** PLUS my
Cash Reward. I understand that I am under no
obligation to buy anything, as explained
on the back of this card.

168/368 XDL GLYM

Please Print

FIRST NAME

LAST NAME

ADDRESS

APT.#   CITY

STATE/PROV.   ZIP/POSTAL CODE

NO PURCHASE NECESSARY!

K-N16-FMC15

he wanted more, always more. And lucky for them both, tonight would be no different.

Lucius arrived to Naomi's an hour later with two large paper bags with dinner. And from the looks of it, she'd had time to shower and change because she was dressed in a silk lounge set. He was aware of how the fabric clung to her hips and the low V-cut of the top showed him she wasn't wearing a bra. Her nipples were easily visible underneath.

Naomi pulled him inside. "Come in. I'm famished."

Once in the brightly lit hallway, Lucius's eyes once again zoomed to her breasts. "I hope you don't answer the door like that for everyone," he murmured huskily.

"Only for you." She took the bags from him and began walking down the hall.

Lucius had no choice but to follow her and enjoy the view of her silk pajama bottoms. The outline of her firm behind was clear and he knew she couldn't be wearing anything other than a thong. His mouth watered at the thought that his sweet Naomi was pretty much naked underneath the ensemble except for that tiny piece of fabric. He was going to have difficulty not jumping her bones before dinner.

He joined her in the kitchen and watched her from the doorway as she seamlessly pulled out wineglasses, plates and flatware and laid out the spread of pasta and salad he'd brought for them.

"I hope you don't mind, I brought a little bit of everything."

She glanced up with a smile. "It looks great and I'm starved. Care to open the wine?"

After he'd taken care of the cork, he poured them each a glass and they took it, along with their plates heaped with pasta and salad, to Naomi's adjoining dining room. They filled each other in on their days since the last time they'd seen each other nearly twelve hours ago.

It had seemed like an eternity to Lucius. He'd wanted to call her all day but hadn't wanted to appear too eager, so he'd waited until later afternoon. Had she been thinking the same?

"Care to share your disappointment from earlier?" he inquired.

Naomi shook her head. She couldn't tell him that her last hope of saving her company had fallen through. She didn't want to ruin the evening with talk of business. *What difference would it make anyway? Would it change the result?* She'd run out of options, and Lucius had the advantage.

"All right," Lucius said slowly, "if you're sure."

"I'm sure." She dug her fork and spoon into the pasta.

She was thankful when he turned the topic to an art show he'd been invited to. They began discussing art, both classic and modern. Naomi found Lucius to be well versed in not only art, but literature, too, especially when he quoted a poem to her.

"Do you always quote love sonnets to your women?"

His brows furrowed. Lucius couldn't remember ever having done it with anyone else. "No, I don't recall that I have, but you're not one of *my women*."

"Aren't I?" Naomi said with a chuckle, reaching for her wineglass.

Lucius placed his hand over hers, halting her action. "No, you're not. I don't see you that way."

"But—"

He silenced her protests with his index finger. "No *buts*." He reached for her hand and pulled her to her feet. He wasn't ready to share with Naomi exactly what his feelings were, but he could show her. "Come."

He walked her to her bedroom. His eyes were dark with intense desire that only Naomi could quench. When they made it to her bed, the depth of his attraction for her took over. They undressed quickly and Lucius went to work. He kissed every part of her, lingering in certain areas like her navel, the backs of her knees, the undersides of her thighs and finally her womanly nub that was achingly sensitive.

He touched her intimately with his tongue and gripped her hips, lifting them off the bed to bring them closer to his mouth. He pushed her over the edge of control with sweeping thrusts of his tongue at her core. Moans erupted from Naomi's throat. He loved the effect his mouth, tongue and eventually his hands had on Naomi. He wanted to pull everything from her, any resistance she had to him, and make her see that *she* was special, different from the others.

When she gripped his shoulders and held on as if her life depended on it, his tongue dived deeper, penetrating her until she splintered, screaming out his name.

"Lucius!"

He didn't stop; he continued his frenzied quest, using his tongue until she begged him to take her. "Lucius, please."

Only then did he reach for one of the condoms they kept by her bedside table and sheathe himself. Then he was back in place, straddling her hips to enter her in one smooth thrust. Her reaction was instant, and her greedy body milked him. He had no choice but to move, quicker, faster and harder.

Naomi kissed him, winding her legs around his calves, taking him deeper and gripping his buttocks as he rode her. He shuddered inside her as she moved to his rhythm.

When a maelstrom of sensations hit him, Lucius gasped aloud as a tidal wave of pure pleasure surrounded him. He let out a long shout and finally let go. Naomi joined him as her inner muscles clenched tight around him at her own release. The power of his orgasm was so strong it caught Lucius unaware, because the feeling was so foreign, so alien that he wasn't sure he understood its meaning. All he knew was that Naomi was the cause.

Chapter 11

Naomi was scared. Last night, she'd lost herself in Lucius. The feelings, the sensations he evoked when he kissed her, touched her, was buried deep inside her. When she closed her eyes and allowed herself to go there, she could still *feel* him inside her.

Naomi shuddered at the depth of her growing feelings for this man. She didn't want to name it, but she suspected she was falling in love with the tycoon.

"Ms. Brooks, Ms. Johnson is here to see you," her assistant, Sophie, said from the intercom, interrupting Naomi's thoughts.

"Send her in."

Naomi was rising to her feet when Kelsey opened the door.

"Hey, stranger. I didn't expect to see you here," Naomi said, strolling toward her best friend. "What brings you by?"

"I do work here," Kelsey said, waddling farther into the room. In the last couple of weeks her partner had blossomed. Her belly protruded in the maternity jeans and tunic she wore, and her cheeks were round and ruddy.

Naomi smiled. "Of course you do. You've just been cutting back on your hours, as you should," she added, "so I'm just surprised, that's all, and you didn't bring Bella."

"Darryl said he was having trouble replicating the sample I sent him, and I couldn't bring Bella—you know she'd be into *everything*," Kelsey responded.

"The one you cooked up in your kitchen a few weeks ago?"

"One and the same, so I thought I'd come in and lend a helping hand," Kelsey stated, rubbing her belly.

Naomi frowned. "Are you sure that's a good idea? I mean, you are in your last trimester."

"And everything is going fine," Kelsey stated. "I still have two more months to go. You and Owen need to stop worrying. I mean, I know I had a difficult pregnancy with Bella, but I've been feeling great this time around. The morning sickness was nothing like with Bella."

Naomi remembered that all too well. Kelsey had been intent on working for as long as she could until her due date, but her first pregnancy had been riddled with problems, the worst being her hyperemesis gravidarum. She'd had such a severe form of morning sickness, with constant vomiting, crippling weakness and dehydration, that she had taken a leave of absence.

"I'm glad to hear that, Kels," Naomi responded, "but you should still take it easy."

"And I will. While my mother is watching Bella, I'm going to get a couple of hours in downstairs in the lab. I just want to be sure he gets it right. I slaved on the stove a long time to get just the right scent."

Naomi released a long sigh. "Only if you're sure." She was hesitant to allow Kelsey to work at the office instead of her home, this late in her pregnancy. Her gut told her it wasn't the best decision.

"Yes, I'm sure," Kelsey tried to reassure her.

"Well, get on down to the lab before your mom starts calling you that Bella has gotten into her makeup bag again and we'll talk later." There was so much they needed to discuss, primarily her burgeoning relationship with Lucius, if she could call it that. And more.

Kelsey gave her a suspicious look. "All right. I'll stop in before I leave."

Once her door closed, Naomi trotted to her large executive chair and plopped down. Kelsey had known something was wrong and uncharacteristically decided to let the matter drop. And thank God she had. Naomi wasn't looking forward to telling Kelsey the other reason for her distress—she was no closer to raising the money to buy her out than she'd been a month ago when she'd returned from Anaheim. In that short time, her financial team had arranged for meetings with three separate banks and all of them had turned her down. Not a one of them was willing to take a risk on her.

It reminded Naomi of when she and Kelsey were first starting out and no one would loan them the money. The only difference was back then, it had been her and Kelsey against the world, but now she was alone—and she had run out of options.

"Naomi was turned down for yet another loan yesterday," Adam said when he walked into Lucius's office later that afternoon wearing the latest in designer men's suits. The look of pure glee and satisfaction in his eyes as he rubbed his hands together made Lucius feel slightly ill. And why was that? Adam was only doing what *he'd* asked. He was trying to get Lucius Brooks and Johnson.

"Is that right?" Lucius inquired as he put down his pen. "And how many does that make now?"

"Three since she first started inquiring," Adam stated as he sat in one of the two leather chairs opposite Lucius, unbuttoning his suit jacket.

Lucius nodded. Naomi failing to find the necessary funds to buy out Kelsey should have excited him, but instead he felt apprehensive. Brooks and Johnson meant everything to Naomi, and if she lost it, it would kill her.

Since when had he started to care about her feelings? Since he'd begun sleeping with her, Lucius thought to himself. Ever since they'd become lovers, Lucius was beginning to feel different about his quest to obtain Brooks and Johnson.

"What's wrong?" Adam inquired. "I thought this was what you wanted—Naomi on the run. Well, she is now. And with Kelsey's baby due in a couple of months, her back is against the wall."

"Nothing's wrong," Lucius responded, rising from his chair. "I'm just not sure that taking over Brooks and Johnson is what I want anymore."

"Since when?" Adam folded his arms across his chest. "You've been singularly focused on acquiring this company's stock for months, and *now* you're not interested? That's not the reason at all."

"Oh, no? And what's the reason?"

"Naomi. You have the hots for the woman, and it's making you soft. I don't know if you've acted on your attraction, but maybe if you did, you'd get back to having that killer instinct you've always had."

Lucius remained silent, because Adam had hit the nail on the head. An image of Naomi popped inside his mind and he could feel his member get thick. If just thinking about her caused this kind of reaction, then he was hot for her—more than that, he craved her.

"Wait a sec." Adam sat forward in the chair with his

feet planted firmly on the ground. "You've already acted on your lust for the woman, haven't you?"

"A gentleman never kisses and tells."

Adam snorted. "You don't have to tell. I know you, Lucius. And you've hit that." He stared Lucius directly in the eye. "And if I'm on the money, more than once."

Lucius swallowed hard. He hated the way Adam was talking about Naomi, like she was one of the women he usually spent time with who wanted his money, power and fame. Naomi was nothing like them. She was beautiful and sexy, yes, but she was genuine with a kind heart.

"I don't want to talk about this anymore."

"Why, because I dare to call you out on your bull?" Adam inquired. "Fine, have it your way." He rose from the chair, rebuttoning his suit jacket, and started toward the door. "The only reason I've been hell-bent on getting you Brooks and Johnson was because that's what you said you wanted. Why don't you let me know when you're ready to get back down to business, all right?"

Lucius snorted when Adam closed the door behind him. If anyone else had dared to speak to him like that, they'd have been fired on the spot, but Adam was his closest friend and the only person other than his grandma Ruby that he would allow to talk to him any kind of way.

Speaking of his grandmother, he hadn't seen her in weeks. It was time he paid her a visit. And maybe talking to her would help him put his priorities back in order and figure out why he was losing his edge where Naomi was concerned. There was no place in his life for more than a casual fling. Or at least that's what he told himself, but the harder he clung to the thought and denied what he wanted, the more his body betrayed him, as it had done just now with Adam.

Yes, he would go to talk to his grandmother and get some perspective.

* * *

"Naomi, come quick." Darryl's voice came through the intercom.

"Darryl, what is it? What's wrong?" Naomi asked when she picked up the receiver.

"It's Kelsey. She's bent over in pain. I think something is wrong," the chemist said from the other end of the line.

He never got to finish his sentence because Naomi had already dropped the phone and was racing toward the laboratory. Naomi didn't even bother with the elevator; instead she took the stairs two at a time from the fourth floor to the first. She ran down the hall to the lab, where she found Kelsey seated on a chair, hyperventilating.

"Kelsey." Naomi rushed to her side and fell to her knees. "What is it?"

Tears were streaked down Kelsey's cheeks, and her face was flushed pink. "It's the baby, Naomi. Something's wrong."

Naomi took Kelsey's hand in hers and gave it a gentle squeeze. It was cold and clammy. "It's going to be fine, okay? Did you call an ambulance?" She looked up at the chemist.

"Yes, of course. As soon as she started having contractions," he answered.

"Contractions?" Naomi's eyes grew large as she looked into Kelsey's baby blues. "Kels—are you sure?"

Kelsey shook her head. "Yes, no, I don't know. But it's just so painful." Just then another pain must have stabbed Kelsey in the abdomen, because she cried out, doubling over in pain. "Oh, my God, this can't be happening now. It's too soon, Naomi. It's too soon."

Naomi was worried. Why hadn't she gone with her instincts and sent Kelsey home when she'd arrived? And now look at her. "Breathe, baby girl. Breathe." Naomi mimicked the breathing techniques they'd practiced during Lamaze class. "C'mon, breathe with me. One. Two."

Her calmness was enough to begin to quiet Kelsey's hysteria until the ambulance arrived a few minutes later. As they placed her in the back, Kelsey held Naomi's hand tightly. "Please don't leave me."

"Of course not, sweetie," Naomi stated. "I'm with you." She joined Kelsey in the back of the ambulance as they shut the double doors. She squeezed Kelsey's hand. "I'm here for you. Right here with you."

Lucius arrived at his grandmother Ruby's house later that afternoon and found her sitting outside on her large wraparound porch, crocheting in her rocker. He'd tried unsuccessfully to move her to a nicer home in a better neighborhood, but she'd been stubborn and told him this was her home and she wasn't going anywhere.

"Lucius?" his grandmother called out to him after he'd parked and approached the house.

"Yes, it's me, Grandma." He climbed the steps of the porch and came to her side.

Ruby Turner wasn't an average grandmother and didn't sit at home waiting to get older. She walked several miles a day and had an active social life, attending church and her women's group functions. Lucius supposed that's why she'd been able to maintain her figure. At eighty-two, she was still as slender and spry as when he'd come to live with her when he was nine years old and had gotten kicked out of one too many boarding schools. She dressed in the latest fashions, thanks to the generous stipend he placed in her bank account each month. There was no way his grandma would live off Social Security benefits alone. With her smooth café au lait complexion, Ruby didn't look a day over sixty.

"You're looking beautiful as always," Lucius said just before he kissed her on the cheek.

"Oh, you charmer you." She waved her hand at him. "Come sit with me and have some sweet tea."

His grandmother's answer for everything was a jug of her famous sweet tea. He supposed it came from her having been raised in Georgia before moving out west because his grandfather worked in the shipping business.

"Sweet tea sounds great, Grandma." Lucius joined her in the adjacent rocker next to hers. He watched her pour the tea into a mason jar. "Thanks." He accepted the jar and took a sip. "Just as good as I remember."

"I'm a Georgia peach," his grandmother responded with a smile. "Of course I know how to make sweet tea. But enough about me. What brings you by in the middle of a workday?"

Lucius gave her a sideways glance. "Can't I just come by to visit my grandma?"

She threw her head back and laughed. "C'mon, Lucius. I raised you. Don't you think I know when there's something on your mind?"

He shrugged. "I suppose."

"Then out with it. I don't have all day."

Lucius laughed to himself. Of course, she didn't, his grandma stayed busy. "There's this woman."

"Of course," she murmured, "it had to be a woman."

He glared at her, but then his grandmother gave him the evil eye and he quickly corrected his look before she backhanded him. "The thing is, I've been seeing this woman. Naomi's her name."

"And?"

"And she has me twisted, Grandma," Lucius stated, leaning back in his chair. "The only reason I sought her out was because I wanted her company, but when I met her—I don't know. Something just kind of clicked. And we kind of fit together, ya know?"

"And that scares you," his grandmother finished, judging the situation rightly. "Your feelings for this woman?"

He nodded. "How did you know?"

"You've always held your emotions in check, Lucius. You have since the moment you came to live with me. Nothing and no one could get to you. You wouldn't let them. You've built walls so high and so thick, but I always knew it was just a matter of time before someone would break through the barriers you have erected around your heart."

"I don't know about all that," Lucius said. "All I'm saying is that I'm conflicted. I wanted her company and…"

"And now you might want the lady instead?"

"I dunno. Maybe. It's too soon to tell. All I know is she's causing me to feel all these emotions that I've never wanted. And I don't know what to do about them."

His grandmother eyed him suspiciously, as if she didn't believe a word that was coming out of his mouth.

"Why are you looking at me like that?"

"What are you so afraid of, Lucius?" his grandmother asked. "Of loving someone? Of being loved?"

"I love you," he returned.

"That's not the same and you know it," she said softly. "Is it because of your mama? Did she damage you that much that you can't allow yourself to be happy and to love this woman?"

Lucius's cell phone vibrated in his jacket pocket and he reached for it. It was Adam. "Yes?"

"I don't know if you're interested in this news, but I reached out to Owen Johnson to talk about the selling his wife's shares and he informed me that Kelsey was taken by ambulance to Long Beach Memorial Hospital. If ever there was a time to strike while the iron is hot, it's now. If the stress of work—"

Lucius didn't allow Adam to finish his sentence and ended the call. He rose from the rocker and started for the steps. "I'm sorry, Grandma. I have to go. It's an emergency and can't be helped."

"Wait!" She jumped from her recliner as fast as she could and rushed toward him. She grabbed both sides of his face in her small palms. "Lucius, if you're starting to fall for this woman, don't run away from it. Embrace it. You'll never know just how much joy love can bring into your life if you're not willing to allow it in."

He nodded and then bounded down the porch steps to his Bentley. He had to get to the hospital. To Naomi. She would need him.

Chapter 12

"This is all your fault," Kelsey's husband, Owen, yelled at Naomi as soon as he saw her in the hospital corridor.

Naomi was so taken aback, she could only stand there in shocked disbelief. She'd just left Kelsey's side and was stepping outside to handle some Brooks and Johnson business when Owen attacked.

"You're the reason Kelsey's in there." He pointed to the hospital room behind him.

"Listen, Owen, I know you're upset."

"Upset?" His voice rose. "I'm furious. Kelsey had no business being at the office. You and I both know that the doctor told her to take it easy with this pregnancy after her two miscarriages and difficult pregnancy with Bella, but you just couldn't let it rest, could you?" He circled around her, letting all of his anger and rage out on her.

Naomi was strong enough to take it, because she knew she'd done nothing wrong. She hadn't asked Kelsey to come to the office. In fact, she'd advised her to leave, but Kelsey had a mind of her own and was going to do what she wanted to. But Naomi wasn't about to tell Owen that—not when he was enraged.

"You had to get her all riled up when you reminisced about the past and how you both started the business. But things have changed, Naomi. It isn't just you and Kelsey against the world anymore. Kelsey is a wife. She has a family and husband and people who need her. I know that might be hard for you to understand since you've always been alone, but—"

Owen never got to finish his sentence, because Lucius stepped in between them.

"Now wait just a darn minute," Lucius said, facing the red-faced man who'd been bullying Naomi when he arrived on the maternity floor. He'd expected they'd be pulling together in a time of crisis, but instead the man was unleashing his hurt on Naomi. It wasn't fair. But she was just standing there, taking it. It made him respect her even more, because she refused to kick a man when he was down. "This isn't Naomi's fault."

"Isn't it? She's the reason my wife was in the lab because she was afraid to let go and allow Kelsey to sell her shares."

"Naomi is not responsible for Kelsey's condition. Now what you need to do is calm down and then go in there—" he pointed to the door "—and be with your wife."

Owen huffed but didn't speak another ill word to Naomi as he entered his wife's room.

Lucius pulled Naomi aside and touched her arm. "Are you okay?" He searched her eyes for a sign that Owen had upset her.

"Y-yes, I'm fine." She stared back at him. "But you, what are you doing here? How did you know?"

Lucius wasn't about to tell Naomi that Adam was speaking with the Johnsons on his behalf. "I called your office and asked for you. Sophie told me you were in the hospital."

Naomi nodded, accepting his answer. "Well, thank you for that." She glanced at the door Owen had just disappeared behind.

"Why in heaven's name were you allowing him to speak to you that way? If I hadn't gotten here when I did, he would have decimated you."

"I—I don't know…" Tears immediately formed in her eyes, and he could see her blinking them back, trying to keep them at bay, so he slid his arms around her shoulders and brought her closer to him.

"It's all right, baby," he crooned softly in her ear as he rubbed her back. "It's okay. I've got you."

Later, once she'd calmed down, Naomi sat with Lucius in the waiting room. He'd gone to the cafeteria earlier to get her some dinner, which now sat uneaten in the disposable container it came in. Naomi didn't have an appetite—not after everything that had happened.

Kelsey being rushed to the hospital and Owen unloading his anger at her. Thank God for Lucius. If he hadn't gotten there when he did, who knew what other hurtful words would have spewed from Owen's mouth. But she would never tell Kelsey what went down. Her friend was battling to keep her baby in her womb.

Naomi had never been so frightened in her entire life. Despite what Owen thought, she would never want anything to happen to the baby and Kelsey. So what, Naomi couldn't hang on to her company? Naomi wasn't that superficial. She valued her friendship, her sisterhood with Kelsey more than any company. She hoped Kelsey knew that and resolved to tell her just as soon as she could.

"It's okay," Lucius said, breaking into her thoughts. She felt his firm grip on her trembling hands.

Naomi turned to him. "Thank you for being here."

"You don't have to keep thanking me."

"Well, I'm sure this is not how you wanted to spend your evening."

"Don't presume to know what my plans were," Lucius said sharply. "I *want* to be here."

Naomi was surprised by the stern tone in his voice. He *meant* what he said, and she believed him. Did that make her a fool? Was he playing her so he could get closer to her and to Kelsey? "I won't presume," she finally responded, "and I'm sorry. It's been a long, emotionally taxing day."

"You don't have to apologize, either," Lucius said softly. "Your best friend and partner suffered a scare, but I'm positive that everything is going to be okay."

Naomi glanced down the corridor. "If I didn't know any better, I'd purposely think Owen is not updating me on Kelsey to spite me."

"I wouldn't put it past him."

"Excuse me for a moment." Naomi rose and stepped away from the waiting area. She used her smartphone to call Kelsey's mother, who was at home with Bella.

Several minutes later, she returned to the waiting area and Lucius looked up from his iPhone. "Everything okay?"

"Oh, yes." Naomi slid next to him in the low-backed chair. "Kelsey's mom told me she's doing good and the contractions have stopped."

"That's wonderful news."

Lucius didn't get a chance to continue, because Naomi saw Owen walking toward them. She inhaled sharply and steeled herself for another attack.

When he reached her, Owen said stiffly, "Against my better judgment, Kelsey has asked to see you."

Naomi jumped up and rushed out of the chair. She was nearly down the hall when she remembered Lucius and he mouthed, *go*.

Upstairs in the maternity ward, Naomi was so excited to see Kelsey, she immediately started crying tears of joy when she entered the room.

"Please don't cry," Kelsey exclaimed as Naomi rushed toward the bed to gingerly sit before pulling her friend into a hug. "I'm okay." She returned her hug.

Naomi pulled away and looked into Kelsey's blue eyes. "Are you sure? You gave us such a fright."

Kelsey nodded. "Gave you a fright? Lord, I thought Owen's head was going to explode. But I'm fine. The medication appears to be working, because the contractions have stopped."

"I'm so relieved." Naomi scooted backward onto the edge of the bed. "Owen wasn't too happy with me."

"Was he terribly dreadful?"

Naomi waved her hand dismissively. She would never say a word to Kelsey about how abominably he'd behaved. She had enough to deal with. "Nothing I couldn't handle."

Kelsey sighed. "He was just scared, Naomi, as am I. And—" She paused as if trying to find the right words, but Naomi already knew what she was going to say.

"And that's why you're going to sell your remaining shares?" Naomi finished.

Tears welled in Kelsey's eyes, and she nodded her head. "I'm so sorry, Naomi. I wanted to give you more time to raise the capital. But I can't turn down what Knight International is offering me. It is well above market value and this would secure *my* future, *my children's* futures. Please don't be upset with me."

Naomi reached for Kelsey's hand across the thin hospital blanket. "Don't worry about me, Kelsey. I'll be fine. You have to take care of you and this baby." She touched her rounded belly. "That's all that matters."

"But if I sell, Lucius will have majority interest in the company." Kelsey sniffed, wiping away her tears with the back of her hand.

Naomi patted Kelsey's thigh. "You let me worry about that."

She wouldn't belie her fears about what Lucius's take-over of her company might mean. Would she be out as CEO? Would he want to make sweeping changes? Would her staff lose their jobs? Somehow, someway, Naomi would figure it out with the man she now realized she'd fallen hopelessly in love with. She had to. Otherwise she would end up shattered because she'd let the playboy tycoon into her heart.

Chapter 13

"I heard from Kelsey Johnson," Adam told Lucius as they played basketball at the fitness center inside Knight International's offices a couple of days later. Encouraging a healthy lifestyle was important to Lucius, which was why he'd installed a state-of-the-art gym in the headquarters, complete with exercise and weight equipment, racquetball, and group fitness classes. He supported his employees' goals for living long, healthy and productive lives.

"Oh, yeah?" Lucius tried to act nonchalant as he dribbled the ball toward the basket.

Adam blocked him, so Lucius did a fake to the right before spinning around left to shoot the ball. The basketball slid easily inside. Nothing but net.

Adam ran over to rebound the ball and caught it before Lucius could get there. "She's ready to sell," he continued, "I think that hospital incident scared her and her husband. We already own 30 percent of Brooks and Johnson—with Kelsey's shares, we're poised to own 55 percent of Brooks and Johnson. You just have to tell me if you're ready to pull the trigger, but the company is yours for the taking."

Lucius took advantage of Adam's chattiness to steal the

ball from him and fast-break down the court to the other side. He rushed the net and did a quick layup.

"Son of a—" Adam yelled when he finally made it down the court, slightly out of breath.

"You snooze, you lose," Lucius laughed.

"Ha-ha," Adam responded. "You still haven't answered my question. I think your play was a way to deflect my attention away from the matter at hand."

Lucius stopped dribbling and snatched the ball up. "And what's that?"

"Your inability to make a decision where this company is concerned because of your latent feelings for its owner."

"I don't have feelings for Naomi." As soon as the words were out of his mouth, Lucius knew they were a lie. He'd been struggling for weeks with his feelings for the woman, and then the other night his protective side had come out. His instinct to protect someone close to him was usually reserved for his grandmother. Needless to say, he was confused by his actions. He'd been ready to beat Owen to a bloody pulp for hurting Naomi.

"Lie to me all you want," Adam responded, "but stop lying to yourself, man. You need to figure out how you feel about Naomi and if you want the relationship to lead somewhere."

Lucius frowned. "Lead where?"

Adam shrugged. "I don't know. To what normal people want. Marriage. Babies. A house. All that. Because, trust me, that's the type of woman Naomi is. She's not the usual woman you've dated and discarded, Lucius. She's the kind of woman you marry."

Lucius thought about Adam's words long after their basketball session ended at the gym and he was drinking a glass of scotch on the balcony of his penthouse.

Adam was right. He was torn. Torn between being the

ruthless corporate raider he'd always been and the man he was with Naomi. When he was with her, he was different, felt different. He needed more time. He had to take Adam and his grandmother's advice and figure out exactly where he stood with Naomi.

A thought sprang into his head, and he had the answer. Now he just hoped that Naomi would go along with it. If not, he would have to use persuasive measures to convince her.

Naomi felt sick to her stomach after meeting with Tim to review her finances. It was done. There was no way she would have enough capital to buy out Kelsey. She would have to leverage all the profit she'd made, wipe out nearly all her savings and mortgage her house to buy Kelsey out. If Brooks and Johnson's stock suffered or the company had any setbacks, she would feel the brunt of it as major stockholder. Was being in charge that important to her that she would risk her entire nest egg and her home?

Naomi was grappling with the question when her cell phone rang. She glanced down and saw it was Lucius.

Why did he have to call now when she was a wreck?

If she ignored the call, he would just call her personal line at the office.

She quickly reached for her phone and swiped to answer. "Hello, Lucius."

"Naomi. How are you? How's Kelsey?"

Naomi released a long sigh. So this call was about Kelsey and her shares, not about her. "I'm fine, and Kelsey's been released from the hospital and is at home resting comfortably."

"That's wonderful," Lucius responded.

"Yes, I'm relieved. Though Owen may not believe it, I only want the best for Kelsey."

"That guy is a real jerk. Although I'd like to use another word to describe him."

Naomi laughed. "I echo that sentiment. So, what's the purpose for your call?"

"Do I have to have one?" Lucius replied.

"No, I just—" Naomi sighed. Figuring out her finances was her problem; Lucius had always been honest with his intentions and his desire to buy B and J. She just wasn't sure how to handle losing controlling interest in her company to the man she was in love with. "It's just been a long day. What's up?"

"I wanted to invite you up to my cabin at Big Bear. I thought perhaps we could enjoy some skiing or perhaps a dip in the hot tub as we look at the stars. What do you say?"

Joy raced through Naomi. Lucius wanted to spend uninterrupted time with her? What did it all mean? There was only way to find out. "Yes, I would love to," she responded.

"Great!" She heard the smile in Lucius's voice at her acceptance. "If you can get off a bit early, we could leave tomorrow morning before traffic gets bad and have more of the weekend."

"Sure. I'm the boss, so I can take the day off."

When they ended the call several minutes later, Naomi was brimming with excitement. Deep down, she wanted more from Lucius, but she was too afraid to allow herself to go there. But now, they would spend the entire weekend together. Perhaps after that Naomi would know once and for all how Lucius truly felt about her and whether he wanted her, the company or both.

As Lucius drove to Naomi's house the next morning, he didn't feel an ounce of nerves. Of one thing he was certain—he enjoyed Naomi. He couldn't wait to get her underneath him and would waste no time doing so. He'd been battling his desire for her and his ambition with ensuring Knight International was a force to be reckoned with.

He was hoping the weekend would give him clarity. Show him what it was he truly wanted from Naomi. Was she just a very sexy outlet for his overzealous libido? Or was there more, as his grandmother and Adam had said? Regardless, he couldn't wait to have his way with her. And they would have the entire weekend with no interruptions, at least not on his end. He'd told Adam in no uncertain terms that he was MIA for the weekend and to call him at his own risk. It had better be something just short of a tsunami for him to disturb him. He had plans for Naomi Brooks.

When he arrived at Naomi's, she was already packed and looking hot. She was wearing a cream-colored sweater with a scarf around her neck and skinny jeans that showed off her slim but curved in all the right places figure.

"Hey, babe." He reached for Naomi, circling his arm around her waist so he could bring her closer for a kiss. She didn't pull away and instead grabbed both sides of his face and kissed him full and deep on the mouth, returning his ardor.

They pulled away several moments later. "Hi." She smiled up at him.

That's when Lucius knew it was going to be one helluva weekend.

The drive to Big Bear went smoothly since they'd gotten a jump start on traffic on 91 east and Interstate 10. During the scenic drive into the San Bernardino National Forest and passing the snowcapped mountains, Naomi regaled Lucius with tales of her family road trips, songs, mishaps and generally how much fun they'd had. It made Lucius a bit envious to hear her family stories when he had none to share of his own. He and Grandma Ruby had never vacationed. And the only time he'd traveled was the odd trip to visit his mother in whatever new villa or penthouse she was staying at abroad, none of which had ever amused Lucius. After a time, Jocelyn had stopped sending for him.

Eventually, they made it to the cabin he'd rented for the weekend.

"You call this a cabin?" Naomi asked, looking up at the house as he unloaded their bags from the trunk.

Lucius had to admit the travel agent had outdone herself. The grand driveway entrance led to an impressive log and stone chalet on top of a hill that overlooked Big Bear Lake. And this was just the outside. He couldn't wait to see what the inside looked like.

"This is more like a château. And this place is beautiful and it smells of wood smoke," Naomi commented, wiggling her nose.

"That's because I ensured they started the wood-burning fireplace for us, so we could get cozy and out of this cold."

Naomi shivered. "It is pretty chilly. The weatherman said the high here was only going to be thirty degrees today."

"That means we'll have to find other ways to keep warm." Lucius gave her a conspiratorial wink. "C'mon, let's get inside."

When he opened the door of the chalet and dropped their bags, they both stared at the sheer size and beauty of this cabin. There were windows everywhere, and large glass doors gave them a spectacular view of the town.

"This is breathtaking." Naomi walked on the rich wood-planked floor of the main living area toward the windows and deck that overlooked the mountains. She paused on the way, stepping over the bearskin rug to finger the elaborate stone wall that held a large flat-screen TV and fireplace below it.

Lucius followed and came behind her to circle his arms around her waist. "I'm glad you like." He glanced behind him at the rug and couldn't wait to make good use of it.

Naomi spun around in his arms. "I *love* it!" She circled her arms around his neck, and he leaned forward to brush his lips across hers.

They continued touring the lower level of the home, ooh and aahing over each new discovery.

The main living area had big comfy camel sofas, handmade wooden tables and a poker table, but the best was yet to come. They found an in-home movie theater with reclining seats and a game room, which had a pool table and built-in stone bar. Lucius doubted though they would be using the movie room, as he intended to keep Naomi on her back much of their visit. He had a lot to work through. Only then could he could make sense of these feelings he was having.

There was a state-of-the-art kitchen with stainless steel appliances, rich oak cabinetry, granite countertops and even a cappuccino machine. The kitchen led to a deck on the main level, which included a large Jacuzzi. Lucius planned to make good use of it. The upstairs was just as spectacular as the downstairs. The master bedroom had the same matching stone wall with fireplace and television and its own deck with a panoramic view. The bathroom was a modern marble masterpiece, complete with sunken Jacuzzi tub, walk-in rainfall shower and dual vanities.

"What would you like to do now?" Naomi asked once they were back in the master suite.

Lucius grinned wolfishly.

"Besides that," she said with a smile. "That's later."

"Promise?"

A wide grin spread across her lips. "Oh, absolutely. You *will* get lucky tonight."

And Lucius couldn't wait.

Naomi was having the time of her life. She didn't know it was possible to feel this relaxed, yet excited all at the same time. After she and Lucius had toured the house, she'd thought they'd need to go out for provisions. But when she'd looked in the double-sided refrigerator and pantry, she found Lucius had ensured they were fully stocked, including liquor. It was like he'd prepared for the zombie apocalypse.

He'd humored her and they'd gone into town to walk around Big Bear Village to find someplace for dinner. She knew what was on his mind. He'd been ready to take her to bed the instant they arrived. She'd seen the hungry look in his eye when they'd stood in the master bedroom and she'd asked what he wanted to do next. She'd wanted the same thing, but she'd never been to Big Bear and wanted to see some of the town before they indulged in extracurricular activities.

Lucius held her hand as they walked down Main Street side by side, popping into the odd shop or just windowshopping. Or in Lucius's case, actually buying something. Naomi was shocked when he pulled her inside a jewelry store and bought her a diamond pendant necklace.

They ended the evening at Madlon's, a local familyowned French restaurant. They both ordered something different so they could try each other's food. Naomi's duck dish was simply divine, but she equally liked Lucius's veal dish with mustard sauce. They chatted and talked while enjoying dessert and an after-dinner drink.

She indulged and plopped a sweet and sticky treat into her mouth and was looking for a napkin to wipe her fingers, when Lucius reached for her hand and took each sticky finger into his own mouth and suckled on them.

Her reaction was swift. Naomi thought she'd implode with desire and drew in a deep breath at the sheer delight of having Lucius's mouth around her fingers.

Times like these amazed Naomi. Lucius wasn't the same man the media made him out to be—this ruthless tycoon with no conscience. She found him to be not only caring, funny and gregarious, but downright romantic. She liked this side of him and wished more people could see it.

"Why are you looking at me like that?" Lucius asked, peering at her strangely. "Is there something in my teeth?" He showed off his pearly whites.

Naomi chuckled. "Nothing so indelicate. I was just thinking that there are many sides to you. Sides you don't share with the world."

He stared solemnly at her and then reached for his wine-glass, taking a sip. "Only with you, it seems."

Naomi didn't know what to make of that. "Does that scare you?"

How intuitive of her, Lucius thought as he stared across at Naomi in the candlelight. That she could pick up on his anxiety where she was concerned. But he'd never been one to show weakness, and he wouldn't now. Not when he hadn't even figured it out himself.

"Of course not," he replied. "It's more surprising than anything. You bring out the best in me, Naomi Brooks."

He loved the wide grin that spread across her beauti-fully shaped mouth. A mouth he couldn't wait to devour. His gaze rested on her pouty bottom lip and he wanted to suck it. Lucius felt his groin begin to ache. "Are you ready to get out of here?" he murmured huskily.

She nodded.

Perhaps she sensed that she'd awakened the animal in him that couldn't be kept at bay any longer.

He quickly dispensed with the bill and they headed to the car. With minimal traffic, they were back at the chalet within minutes.

As soon as the door closed, he covered the ground between them. He crushed Naomi to him, plundering her lips as he'd wanted to do at the restaurant. She matched his hunger and they eagerly undressed in the hall, yanking off their scarves, coats and boots. Once free, Naomi surprised him by jumping into his arms and locking her legs around his waist.

Lucius held her tightly in his arms and carried her upstairs to the master bedroom. Once there, he tossed the duvet cover back and sat Naomi atop. Naomi yanked him by his shirt, pulling him hard against her. When his lips grazed hers, he felt the points of her breasts against his chest, igniting a fire inside him. He licked her lips, seeking entry, and she gave in to him, openly giving herself so he could deepen the kiss. Did she feel the same feverish passion that was rising within him?

He got his answer at her eager surrender of her mouth to him. Excitement seeped through him like wildfire, reaffirming everyone's opinion that he was starting to fall for this beautifully seductive woman. He was consumed by her responsiveness to his kiss and it made their connection more powerful, more real. He'd never been so aroused just from a kiss!

Naomi wanted Lucius more than she'd wanted any other man. She was burning up with the need to have this man inside her.

When he finally tore his mouth from hers, her heart was pumping wildly in her chest. And when his hands went to the hem of her sweater, all she could do was lift her arms so he could rid her of the garment. She wanted to be naked against him. She reached behind her and unclasped her bra, releasing her breasts.

His eyes widened, but that didn't stop him from yanking his sweater over his head in one fell swoop until they were both naked from the waist up.

Naomi reached for his belt buckle, unlatching it and his zipper. Lucius rose from the bed and pulled his pants and briefs free until he stood as naked as the day he was born, and with one hell of an erection. Naomi motioned him over with her index finger. He did as instructed and she unzipped her jeans. Then she fell backward on the bed so Lucius could tug then down her hips and legs and toss them aside.

She wasn't embarrassed wearing only her bikini panties, because the passion glazing Lucius's eyes told her that he wanted to *see her*. She raised her hips and he slid his thumbs along the waistband to slide the delicate fabric over her hips until she was naked.

She scooted farther onto the bed and Lucius crawled up on top of her. The breath whooshed out of her as he lowered his mouth back down over hers while one of his hands spread her legs apart. She welcomed his touch; she was already wet and ready for him and writhed against his searching fingers.

When he lifted his head and saw her dilated eyes, she conveyed without words just how much she wanted him. He leaned over to the nightstand and produced a condom from the box he'd brought and set in plain sight. After he'd sheathed himself, he returned to her. Using his knees to spread her thighs apart, he surged inside her.

They came together in a rush of lust, heat and passion. Their desire-drenched bodies made shadows in the firelight as they ascended the highest peak. Naomi clasped her legs around Lucius's buttocks as they both reached infinity at just the same time and began to free-fall back toward earth.

Chapter 14

Naomi marveled at Lucius's stamina. They'd gone throughout the night and his libido hadn't waned. He'd been able to take them to new heights, and she'd felt waves and waves of sensual pleasure. The morning came slowly, and Naomi awoke first, which allowed her time to watch Lucius as he slept. His body was nestled next to her, one arm resting possessively over her bottom.

Her skin smelled like his musky scent, a heady combination. And a losing battle. She'd fallen in love with Lucius. She knew it was a fool's mistake when he was only using her until his passion for her cooled, but that didn't help with the predicament she'd put herself in. This man she loved had the power to destroy her life's work.

Brooks and Johnson was all she had. And yes, she did have her family to support her, but B and J was her baby. Without it, where would she be?

But where would she be without Lucius?

Just then, he began to stir beside her, pulling her toward him. "Good morning," he said, wiping the sleep from his eyes.

"Good morning."

"Did you sleep okay?"

"I slept like a log after you wore me out."

Lucius smiled sheepishly. "Oh, don't act like you didn't like it."

"Did I?" Naomi responded cheekily.

"How about I remind you." He leaned over her and sought her lips with his own.

While he deepened the kiss, Lucius felt Naomi's hands sliding down his body to find the swell of his penis. Then she shocked him by reaching for the box of condoms on the nightstand and pulling out a packet. He loved that she took it upon herself to protect them. Before he knew it, she'd swiftly moved to straddle him.

He was both surprised and delighted by her boldness. His hands immediately went to her hips to help ease her onto his throbbing erection. He watched her eyes close as she slowly took him inside her body inch by delicious inch. Then she began to torment him with the rise and fall of her body atop his. At times she would come down slowly onto his manhood, other times fast and deep, holding him until he had no choice but to start pumping underneath her. With her hands on his chest, she stopped him.

He understood without her having to speak. That's how attuned they were to each other. This was *her* ride. She was in control.

It was as if a deep ache in Naomi's stomach had to be quenched. She began to ride him faster and faster. When she reached the precipice, she cried out and tremors shook her entire body, causing her to fall on top of him.

Lucius took advantage and flipped her onto her back, rolling her beneath him. This time he was the one in control and thrust inside her in one fell swoop. He took his time making love to her. Cupping her breasts in his hand, he took one sensitive bud into his mouth and suckled while the lower half of his body slowly moved of its own accord. Naomi clutched at muscles in his back with her hands as he climbed them toward infinity.

When he felt convulsions tighten her body and her inner muscles clutched around him, it caused Lucius's own tidal wave of an orgasm to come crashing down. Only then did Lucius give in and surrender himself to its power.

Later that morning after cooking breakfast, Naomi and Lucius set out for a fun day in the snow. Naomi wasn't too keen on skiing, so instead Lucius arranged for them to go snowmobiling and tubing after they'd dressed in several layers due to the bitter cold.

After a scenic chairlift ride to the top, the two of them went down by bobsled on the alpine slide. They each navigated their own sled down a quarter-mile-long cement track. Naomi got a thrill from every twist and turn. And so did Lucius, because he whooped and hollered from his bobsled.

Although it was freezing outside, Naomi couldn't recall having so much with another person. Seeing this light-hearted, fun-loving side to Lucius was more than she could have ever dreamed, and she liked—no, she loved it. Loved him. Armed with the knowledge of her feelings for this incredible man, Naomi did her best to hide how she felt about him. She didn't want Lucius to feel like he had to share them. Her feelings were her own. He'd never offered her anything more than what they'd experienced, and she would just have to be happy with that and live in the moment.

But there was a part of her, in the deep recesses of her mind, that yearned for more. Wished that Lucius shared her feelings. She knew that he enjoyed being with her.

Why else would he have invited her for the weekend? But it was just physical for him. She craved the intimacy that came from true love between a man and a woman. Would she ever find a man that loved her as much as she loved him? Or was Lucius that man and he didn't know it yet?

To warm up, they ended the evening much as they had spent the day, having fun at the Big Bear Lake Brewing Company, where they sampled the restaurant's best craft and microbrews while munching on an assortment of appetizers.

Naomi was stuffing a fry topped with their famous homemade beer-cheese sauce, grilled onions and bacon crumbles in her mouth when she saw Lucius smiling at her. "What's so funny?" she asked with a mouthful of decadent French fry.

"You. You are really something."

Naomi used her napkin to wipe her mouth. "In a good way, I hope?"

Lucius grinned. "Definitely a good way. I doubt I would ever get one of my usual dates to dine on—" he motioned to the monster honey-chipotle wings and beer-cheese fries on the table "—to ever let me take them to someplace so casual. But you, you don't mind at all."

Naomi chuckled. "Well, I don't eat like this *all* the time," she emphasized, "but I don't mind having a beer and wings. I'm not that uppity. Perhaps you've been dating the wrong sort of woman."

Lucius stared at Naomi. She was right. He had been dating beautiful, vain and materialistic snobs who wouldn't be caught dead in a place like this. Let alone accompany him bobsledding and get their ski outfits dirty. Naomi was different. She was down-to-earth and looked darn fine in the outfit he'd purchased for her of a ski jacket with a lambskin collar, turtleneck and snug leggings that hugged her behind just how he wanted it.

He'd enjoyed spending the day with her. It had been nothing short of magical. There was a twinkle in her eye as she'd wholeheartedly gone for whatever activity he suggested. He could be real with Naomi. And she was the only woman he'd opened up to about his past, his lack of a father and his yearning to be part of a family.

She'd gone a step farther by inviting him to her parents' home so he could see what it was like. Lucius had to admit that he wouldn't mind being part of a large family. Maybe then he'd finally feel like he belonged somewhere, to someone. *Someone like Naomi*, an inner voice suggested.

Lucius wasn't ready to admit to that. What he did want to do was go back to their chalet and get Naomi in a skimpy bathing suit so he could indulge in the hot tub on deck. "What do you say we head out?"

"Absolutely." Naomi pushed away the plate of fries. "Otherwise, I'll eat all of these."

He took care of the bill, generously tipping the great waitress, and they headed back to the chalet. "I was thinking we could try out the hot tub," Lucius commented giving Naomi a sideways glance. "What do you say?"

"Sure. I'm game."

Twenty minutes later, Lucius was sitting in his swim shorts waiting anxiously for Naomi. He couldn't wait to see her in her bathing suit.

Naomi exited the master bathroom wearing a feminine ruffled two-piece leopard-print halter bikini and wearing high heels. For some reason, Lucius had expected her to wear a one-piece, so he was pleasantly surprised by her confidence in her figure as she walked toward him. He felt his manhood jump to attention.

"You like?" She spun around to give him a better view

of the itsy-bitsy bottom that showed him more cheek than an average bathing suit.

Lucius's mouth watered. "I love it!"

She beamed with pride, and he could see a blush spread across her breasts. Breasts he couldn't wait to suck in the immediate future.

"Let's go."

They donned thick terry-cloth robes and embarked downstairs to the kitchen, but not before Lucius slid a foil packet into his pocket. He stopped long enough at the countertop to grab the champagne and flutes he'd left out before opening the screen door.

The air was crisp and cold. Steam was already coming up from the bubbling hot tub.

"Ooh, it's so cold out here." Naomi shivered a bit and her breath steamed.

"You won't be cold for long," he said as she eased off her robe. He helped her up the steps and watched her slide in the water. He swiftly tossed aside his robe and climbed in behind her.

The water was warm and bubbling around them. Naomi sat across from him while Lucius took care of popping open the bubbly. He poured them each a glass and handed one to her.

"Thank you."

"To the best day ever," Lucius said, holding up his glass.

A large grin spread across Naomi's face. "To the best day ever."

Naomi was overjoyed as she sipped her champagne and looked at him through her lashes. She couldn't believe Lucius had enjoyed the day as much as she had. It gave her hope. Even though she knew she should be careful and not get carried away by the statement, she did.

It also didn't help that Lucius was looking at her like she was the cherry on an ice cream sundae. The lust in his eyes mirrored the desire that was churning within her. Every time she was around this man, there was an undeniable attraction she couldn't contain.

Lucius set his flute aside on the built-in cup holder. "Come here," he ordered.

Naomi happily obliged and placed her flute on the cup holder nearest her. Then she walked slowly toward Lucius through the swirling bubbles. His legs were open and she walked between them. He grabbed her around the waist and pulled her tight against him seconds before his mouth claimed hers in a searing kiss.

The kiss took her breath away. Naomi wasn't sure if that was his intention, because she fell into his lap at the sheer force of hunger in his kiss. She felt his teeth at her bosom untying the knot that kept her breasts from him, and the skimpy material floated away. Then she felt the cool air against her nipples and then Lucius's hot hands caressing one mound as his wet tongue closed around one nipple. He licked it until it turned into an engorged bud, and Naomi moaned uncontrollably, her head falling back. Then he turned to the other and laved it with his tongue.

When he pulled away, Naomi wanted to cry out for him not to stop, but it was only long enough for him to free her of the matching bottom. He tossed them onto the deck along with his shorts. He reached for his robe, and much to Naomi's surprise, he pulled out a condom and sheathed his bulging erection. He'd thought of everything for this moonlit encounter.

Thank goodness the house was secluded and no one could see them outside in the nude and making love in the hot tub. Not that Naomi cared. She wanted Lucius, right here and right now. When he sat back down and motioned her over, she straddled him and her stomach tightened in anticipation of what she knew was to come. She eased down slowly until he filled her to the hilt, and a low gasp escaped her lips. She thought she was going to ride him, but instead he flipped positions and had her on the back on the steps of the hot tub. He began moving inside her, slowly, gently. Back and forth. Back and forth. She moved with him, squeezing him tightly with her inner muscles until he began to thrust more vigorously.

"Yes, Lucius. Yes, like that!" she cried.

She saw his jaw clench as he tried to resist the sensations. He grabbed hold of her hips and held her in place, slowing down the pace, so he could once again thrust slowly inside her.

The intensity was building, and Naomi couldn't hold on any longer. She was making so much noise, moaning and groaning, someone had to hear them, and when Lucius kissed her deeply, the kiss sent her entire body into a spasm, contracting around his.

Her response triggered Lucius to shudder violently and throw his head back, eyes shut, and he came with a loud shout. "Naomi!"

When their orgasms subsided, Lucius withdrew and sat beside her on the step.

"What are you doing to me, woman." Lucius had lost control and shown no finesse a moment ago. All he could think about was a driving need to lose himself in her. And he'd tried, but Naomi had given as good as she got and matched him in every way.

"Am I supposed to answer that?" she inquired. "Because I could ask you the same thing. This is completely out of character for me."

Lucius turned to stare at her boldly. "So I bring out this side of you?"

Naomi regarded him warily. "Don't get cocky, Lucius Knight. You know you're a good lover. I'm sure I'm not the first woman to tell you so."

She wasn't, Lucius thought, but she was the first to make him glad he was. And that he was the man who could bring out the sexy temptress in Naomi. "Come, we should go inside before we catch a cold."

They returned to the master bedroom and slid under the warm covers. He pulled her sideways into a spoon position so he could wrap his arm tightly around her. Naomi released a happy-sounding sigh, and soon her breathing slowed, telling Lucius she'd fallen sound asleep after great sex.

Sleep eluded Lucius, however. It wasn't just sex between them anymore. Every time he was with Naomi, he *made love* to her. She was unlike any of his usual women, and that scared him. His uncharacteristic behavior and response to her made Lucius see that commitment would be the only solution for a woman like Naomi. Was he ready for that? He came and went as he pleased. He didn't have to answer to anyone. He'd always enjoyed his bachelor lifestyle and hadn't been looking for a change.

Until Naomi.

Naomi had him reevaluating everything he held dear. He was in uncharted territory and had no idea where to go. Those were his last thoughts as he eventually drifted off to sleep.

Brrring. Brrring.

"Lucius." He could feel Naomi pushing his shoulder. "That's your phone."

"Hmm…?" He was luxuriating in lying close to Naomi.

His hand was on her breast and he could register her heart-beat, which had gradually returned to normal after their lovemaking session in the hot tub caused them to retire to the bedroom. He'd wanted to sleep in, have a leisurely morning sexing her like crazy again before they had to get back on the road to Long Beach.

The shrill of the phone continued until Lucius had no choice but to throw the covers back and jump out of bed. Annoyed, he snatched up the phone and without looking at caller ID said, "This had better be good."

"Lucius, I need you."

"Who's this?" Lucius recognized the voice, it was his mother, Jocelyn.

"What do you want? And how did you get this number?" Not many people knew his personal cell phone number other than his grandmother, Adam and Naomi. He'd only ever given Jocelyn his work cell phone, which he'd purposely not brought with him to the cabin. And since their last meeting had been less than pleasant, Lucius hadn't expected to hear from her.

"Something terrible has happened. You'll see. It's all over the news. And I need your help. I called Adam and he told me where you were and gave me your number. He didn't want to, but this is urgent."

"Don't be overly dramatic, Jocelyn."

"This is life and death, and you need to come quick, Lucius. I'm at…" She began rattling details into the phone.

"Wait! Wait!" Lucius searched for a pen, saw one on the desk and rushed over to take down the particulars. "Okay, go ahead."

Seconds later, after she'd given him the information, the phone went dead.

Lucius stared down at the phone in shock. Jocelyn had never asked him for anything, much less his help. And it would have to be serious for Adam to break his confidence and give Jocelyn his personal phone number. Then he frowned.

Uncaring of his nakedness, he walked over to the nightstand to grab the remote. He clicked on the television, whirling the room with light as he turned to the local news. That's when he saw it.

"Socialite Jocelyn Turner was found in bed with married shipping magnate Arthur Knight, who has been rushed to a Los Angeles hospital from what appears to be a massive heart attack."

"Lucius." Naomi was behind him. He glanced down and saw she'd wrapped a sheet around her torso. "What is it? Who is that?"

He turned to Naomi. "I suspect that man is my father."

Naomi was hurt. After watching the news report, she'd wanted to accompany Lucius to the hospital. It was his mother, after all, and she was in one helluva mess, having been caught in bed with a married man. Arthur Knight had a wife and a son. The fact that he'd been having an affair with Lucius's mother would be big local news. And if Lucius's suspicions about Arthur were true, he would need her.

But Lucius didn't want her to go with him. Instead, after they'd showered and dressed, they'd packed in a hurry and fled Big Bear to get back home to Long Beach. And instead of taking Naomi with him, he'd given her a quick kiss on the forehead and dropped her off at home with a terse "I'll call you," which he'd thrown over his shoulder as he'd raced back to his car.

She knew she shouldn't be upset. He was dealing with a lot. On the drive home, he'd called Adam and ordered him to contact their public relations department. Adam must have fussed about it being a Sunday, because Lucius had stated quite clearly he couldn't care less. It still didn't mean that she didn't want to be there to support him. Who would be in his corner?

Tears sprang to her eyes as her love came pouring out with no place to go.

"How bad is it?" Lucius asked Adam when he met him in the hospital garage. He'd driven to the hospital on autopilot. His mind spinning with the knowledge that after all these years, he'd finally found him. His father. Lucius had finally decided to park rather than come through the front entrance, where a throng of reporters had already congregated.

"Pretty bad. Every major news outlet is all over this story," Adam said as he walked into the hospital with Lucius. He was dressed in jeans and a pullover sweater, same as Lucius. Adam grasped his shoulder. "Perhaps you and I should talk before—"

Lucius shrugged off his hand and interrupted him. "No, I have to go now. Where is she?"

"In the waiting room."

"Take me to her."

They marched down the hall toward the waiting area, where Lucius found his mother curled up in a ball in the corner sobbing into a handkerchief. She wasn't in her usual fashionable attire. Instead, she was wearing jeans, a tank and cardigan that she must have thrown on before the ambulance arrived.

"Mother?"

She looked up when she saw him and jumped out of her chair to rush into his arms. "Oh, Lucius. It was so horrible." She sniffed into his shoulder. "And the press.

They're such monsters. Saying all kinds of terrible things. And calling me names."

Lucius patted her on the head. Unsure of how to handle this Jocelyn. "I'm here now. And I'll take care of everything."

She glanced up at him with tearstained cheeks, "Can you help me see him?" Hope evident in her voice.

He took hold of her by the shoulders. "That's not a good idea. You do realize how serious this is? The repercussions of how salacious this story is. You were caught with a married man in bed, they'll think he died during sex."

She jerked away from him. "I don't care about the darn repercussions. I care about Arthur. I want to see him. Matter of fact, I'm going now." She pushed past him.

Lucius glared at Adam before following her quickly down the hall. "Jocelyn, this is not a good idea. Besides, we *need* to talk. I have some questions that *need* answers."

"I don't care about what people think," she replied over her shoulder. "I have to know how he's doing. We can talk later."

When they rounded the corner, they saw a group of people huddled at the end of the hall. The instant they saw his mother, Lucius knew she'd made a critical mistake.

A tall, elegantly dressed woman with a smooth mocha complexion rushed toward his mother.

"You hussy!" she cried. "How dare you show your face here!"

His mother stepped backward, recoiling from the harsh words and Lucius watched the whole scene play out as if he was an observer instead of a participant. "And look who you brought with you? Arthur's bastard son!"

Chapter 15

Lucius nearly choked when he heard aloud what he'd begun to suspect as he drove back from Big Bear. His mother had been caught in bed with *married* shipping magnate Arthur Knight. *His* last name was Knight. How had his investigators missed their affair? During their research, they'd found no connection between Jocelyn Turner and Arthur Knight. Clearly, they'd been good at covering up their deception.

But now, he finally knew his biological father's identity.

Lucius stared wide-eyed at the woman and then turned to his mother.

"Oh, don't act like you didn't know," the woman continued. "You and your harlot of a mother have been basking in Arthur's money for years."

"Mother." A tall, caramel-toned, clean-shaven brother with deep-set dark eyes and an athletic physique came forward. He was dressed in dark trousers and pale blue dress shirt. "What do you mean for years? Are you saying Dad has another son?" The shock in the man's face was clear, because it mirrored Lucius's. He, too, had no idea what had been going on between his father and Lucius's mother.

The woman turned and caressed her son's face in her delicate slender hands. "I'm so sorry, Maximus, but that's exactly what I'm saying."

"No, it can't be," Maximus responded, glaring in Lucius's direction. "It can't be. Dad wouldn't do that to you. To us."

"It's true, Max," she whispered softly, "and I'm sorry for blurting it out this way, but I couldn't hold it in any longer. Now seeing the evidence—" she motioned to Lucius "—of their affair, right in front of my face. The truth has to be told."

Maximus's face hardened and his eyes turned cold as he looked at Lucius and then at Jocclyn. "That may be true, but you don't need to do this *here* and make a scene. Let's go." He tightened his hand on her arm and began leading her back down the hall, where their remaining group stood in shocked disbelief.

Lucius caught Maximus's long glare before he turned and huddled back with the group.

"Lucius…"

He heard his mother's voice, but it was as if it were in the distance. He couldn't breathe. He had to get out of there.

He blinked several times, trying to clear the fog in his head. "Adam, can you take my mother home, please?"

The look of pity in his best friend's eyes angered Lucius.

"No problem. I'll call you later."

Lucius barely heard a word as he turned on his heel and stormed down the corridor.

"Is everything okay, baby girl?" Naomi's father asked later that evening when she arrived glum faced to their weekly Sunday dinner. She hadn't been in the mood for socializing, but knew if she didn't attend it would raise more suspicions. So instead, she'd arrived an hour early, because she'd wanted some alone time with her father before Gemma and Tim got there. They'd retired to the den while her mother finished dinner.

"Is it because that young fella, Lucius, didn't accompany you?" he inquired.

Naomi shrugged and reached for the chip bowl. She grabbed a large Ruffle and took a generous scoop of onion dip before placing it in her mouth. "Partly," she answered with her mouth full.

Her father mimicked her and she smiled. They'd always been alike. She was a daddy's girl, through and through.

"Talk to me," he said, reaching for another chip. "What's going on?"

"I take it you haven't been watching the news," Naomi replied.

Her father shook his head. "You know Sunday is football day, but eventually I'll get to it. Is there something I should know?"

"No! No one should, but instead Lucius's life is being played out in public, in front of everyone, and I'm powerless to help him."

"What's being played out?"

"The fact that Lucius's mother has been having an affair with a married man."

"Oh."

"That's right. And on top of that, Daddy, he suffered a heart attack while in bed with her and was rushed to the hospital. Lucius barely had time to get dressed before we left Big Bear."

"Big Bear?" Her father's brow rose. "A weekend away sounds awfully romantic, if you ask me."

Naomi waved her hand. "Forget about me right now, if you can, Daddy. I'm worried about Lucius. As soon as he heard about it, he—he changed right in front of me. He became so cold and distant."

"You mean he became the ruthless corporate raider you'd read about?"

She nodded. "But he's never been that way with me. Ever. If you could have seen him this weekend, Daddy. We were having so much fun, laughing, talking, going bobsledding or just enjoying a beer like a normal couple."

"So you admit that you're dating?"

"I don't know if I'd call it that."

"You have to remember that he's not like us, baby girl," her father said, rising to his feet. "He might not have the same life experiences or the coping skills to deal with life's curveballs that I hope I've taught you. I suppose the only way he can deal with all the turmoil is turn off his emotions."

"With me, too?" Naomi knew she sounded weak, but if she couldn't be honest with her father, whom could she be honest with?

"Sometimes we hurt those we love the most."

Naomi snorted. "Love? I doubt that word has ever crossed Lucius's mind when it comes to me, Daddy. I'm just—"

She never finished her sentence, because her father clutched her shoulders. "Don't you dare make light of this, young lady. I taught you better than that. I taught you not only how to love, but that you *deserve* it. And you should settle for nothing less."

Tears welled in her eyes. "I know that, Daddy, I do, but—" She spun away from him. She didn't want him to see her despair.

"You don't think he returns your love?" her father asked.

How had he guessed her feelings? Probably because she was an open book, just as Kelsey had said. She nodded.

He grabbed her chin and turned her to look at him. "I don't know if that's true, baby girl. The man you brought to dinner was head over heels for my daughter."

Naomi shook her head. "You're wrong. He only wants me for sex."

Her father didn't blush at her words. They'd always had an open and honest relationship, and she didn't mince words.

He lowered his head and was silent for several beats. "That may be so, but I also think that young man doesn't know what to do with the feelings he's developing for you. Why? Because he's never had an example. Didn't you tell me he was raised by his grandmother? That his mother has been nonexistent in his life?"

"Yes."

"So, he's never seen real and abiding love between two people until he met me and your mother. It's foreign to him, Naomi. You've got to give him time to come to terms with it. And if what I saw the night you brought him here is true, he'll find his way back to you."

"Do you really think so?"

Her father nodded.

She wanted to believe that Lucius could love her. But was her head in the clouds?

Knock. Knock. Knock.

Naomi wiped the sleep from her eyes. What time was it? She glanced at the watch on her nightstand. It read 2:00 a.m. After coming home from her parents', she'd given up on hearing from Lucius and retired to bed. They'd made it back that afternoon and he'd had plenty of time to go to the hospital, help his mother and still phone her. But he hadn't.

He was showing her exactly what he thought of her. She was good enough for a romp between the sheets on any given day or in a destination of his choosing, but when it came to matters of the heart, he was closed off to her.

That's what she thought, at least, until she padded to the front door and saw a haggard Lucius leaning against the side of her door. His eyes looked haunted, as if he'd seen a ghost. "Lucius?"

"Can I come in?"

"Of course." She grabbed his hand, pulling him inside. She led him to the sofa in her living room, but instead of sitting, he started pacing her wood floor. So she sat with her legs underneath her and waited for him to talk.

"I can't believe it." He shook his head. "I still can't believe it. Even though I heard it with my own ears."

"Believe what?"

"That *I*—" he pounded his chest "—*am Arthur Knight's son.*"

Naomi sucked in a deep breath. Of all the things she'd been expecting to hear, that bombshell wasn't one of them. "What did you say?"

"You heard me. I learned tonight—or should I say yesterday, at the hospital—that I'm Arthur's bastard son. Apparently he and my mother have been carrying on some elaborate affair for over *three*—" he held up three fingers "—*three* decades. How is that even possible? That kind of duplicity? And that she would go along with it? For God's sake, has she no shame?"

Naomi knew he meant it as a rhetorical question and didn't answer. Her heart broke for Lucius. To find out this sort of news like this—so publicly. It was a horrible thing for a mother to do to her son. She should have told him the truth long ago. If Arthur didn't make it, it might be too late.

"Wow!" Lucius finally sat down in the large chair opposite Naomi and held his head in his hands. "I—I don't know what to do with this news, Naomi. What do I do with it?" He glanced at her, and she could see tears glistening in his eyes. "My entire life I've been yearning for the truth, but not like this." He shook his head. "Not like this."

Naomi immediately sprang from the sofa. "Lucius…" She wanted to comfort him, but instead, he gripped her robe by the waist, pulling her to him. She held his head to her body. "I'm so sorry, baby," she whispered as he cried. "I'm so sorry."

She held him, and once he began to quiet, she sat in his lap holding him to her bosom. When he lifted his head, his dark brown eyes were hooded and cloudy with tears. She wiped them away with her hands. "Let me go get you some Kleenex."

She rose, but he grasped her around the waist and brought her back to his lap. "Don't leave me."

Naomi used her index finger to raise his chin. His eyes bored into hers as if they were looking into her very soul. She was startled by the intensity and cast her eyes downward, but Lucius wouldn't let her.

Instead, she felt a tug on her robe as he released it and it fell to her shoulders. Naomi wasn't wearing much, only a satin nightie that showed a fair amount of her cleavage and barely reached her thighs.

Lucius's eyes darkened, turning from hurt and anger to blazing passion. He clutched the back of her neck and brought her lips to his. His mouth was soft and tender at first, but then he steadily increased the pressure, his kiss becoming harder and greedier.

And so were his movements. Naomi felt him reaching between them to unzip his jeans just as he laid Naomi down onto the floor with only her robe to cushion her. He kicked off his shoes and pushed her nightie up and over her head. Then he was kissing and touching and caressing her all over. Causing her entire body to purr with delight.

She heard the tear of a wrapper, but she was too engrossed in the sensual licks of his tongue on her breasts or the nips of his teeth to notice. She only felt. Felt him drive into her. She'd never been taken so strongly before; she couldn't even cry out because all the air had been sucked out of her lungs.

Lucius thrust into her with rapid, deep thrusts that were so intense they consumed her mind, body and soul.

"Lucius…" There was almost a need for him to stop and let her catch her breath, but he was relentless as he awakened her body.

When he reached his climax, Lucius shouted, "Naomi!" and collapsed on top of her.

They lay breathless for minutes, still joined together. Even though she hadn't come, Naomi knew he'd needed the release. Then she felt Lucius swelling inside her. He was *still hard*.

She glanced up at him and grabbed both sides of his face as he started a new tempo. This one was slow with deliberate motions to send her into overdrive so she too could feel sensual bliss. So much so that when they both reached the peak and came spiraling back down to earth, Naomi whispered, "I love you," right before she fell asleep with Lucius in her arms.

Lucius picked Naomi up as she slept, exhausted from his exuberant lovemaking. He carried her to her bedroom and slid her beneath the cool sheets, kissing her forehead.

He shouldn't have come here tonight. It wasn't fair of him to use Naomi as a release for his pain. But instead of calling him out on it, she'd offered herself up to him as a salve. He'd made love to her with such intensity that the depth of their encounter had scared him. As a result, he'd heard words that he'd never thought he'd hear from a woman.

Naomi loved him.

He hadn't imagined it. Although she'd whispered it, he'd heard her loud and clear. Which was why he had to leave. He'd been feeling an emotion some might call love, but it was just a sentiment.

He had no place for love in his life. *Look at me*, he thought. *I'm a disaster. I've a liar for a mother and a cheat for a father. What could I possibly know about love or give to a woman as special as Naomi?*

Picking up his shoes he'd discarded earlier, he quietly tiptoed out of Naomi's house. And maybe out of her life.

Chapter 16

"Hey, man, how you doing?" Adam asked Lucius as he gave him a one-armed hug before walking inside his penthouse later that morning.

"Fine." Lucius closed the door behind him. He'd called his assistant earlier and advised her he would be taking the day off and was accepting no calls.

"I doubt that's true." Adam turned around to face him. "I was there, remember? I heard everything." He watched as Lucius strolled in and sat on the couch.

Lucius rolled his eyes. How could he forget? Hell, the entire hospital had probably learned his mother was Arthur's mistress and he was his illegitimate son. They probably would have learned a lot more if his *brother*, Max—or whatever Latin name they'd called him—hadn't stepped in.

Brother!

He had a brother that he knew absolutely nothing about.

He'd always wanted siblings. A brother or sister, he hadn't cared. He'd just wanted someone to talk to, to confide in, who would be there for him. And all along he'd always had one. But thanks to his parents' deception, he didn't know him. And if the look Maximus Knight gave him at the hospital was any indication, he didn't want to know Lucius, either.

"What can I do? What do you need?"

"Ha!" Lucius laughed out loud and jumped to his feet. "What do I need?" His voice rose. "I needed not to find out who my father was in front of a bunch of strangers! What I needed was for all this to come out years ago when I had time to prepare for the fallout, not when the man has a heart attack."

Adam released a long heavy sigh. "I know that, Lucius. But what's done is done. There is no going back. All we can do now is damage control."

"Why?" Lucius laughed derisively. "I couldn't care less what the world thinks of me. They already think I'm a spoiled playboy, a corporate raider—the title of illegitimate son won't matter much."

"What about your mother?"

Lucius eyes turned cold. "What about her?"

"With Arthur's standing in the community and the business world, the press are going to have a field day with this, Lucius. If they haven't already. This story is juicy and certainly salacious. Not to mention your potential stake in Knight Shipping."

Lucius waved his hand in the air. "I don't want his *money*. I never did."

He shook his head. He couldn't think about that now. He was trying to make sense of the last twenty-four hours.

"I know you don't," Adam replied, "but if something happens to him—"

"Don't you dare." Lucius poked Adam in the chest, "Don't you dare. I can't hear that right now."

Adam threw his hands up in the air. "I'm sorry, all right.

As your friend, I'm just trying to help, Lucius. But I have to tell you, I don't know where to begin."

"Neither do I!" Lucius yelled. "My whole world has been turned on its axis, Adam." He ran his hand over his cropped hair.

Ding. Dong. Ding. Dong.

Lucius stormed toward the door. "I told the guard I wanted no visitors." He swung the door open and found his mother on the other side.

She was wearing all black and sporting a large brimmed hat and sunglasses. She looked more like she was going on vacation than attempting to appear incognito.

"What do you want, Jocelyn?" He held on to the door, keeping her outside in the hall.

"We need to talk."

"That time has long since passed."

She snatched off her sunglasses. "That may be so, but I have some things to say, and you might want to hear them." Being several inches shorter than he, she crouched underneath his arm and strolled inside. "Hello, Adam."

Annoyed, Lucius slammed the door and strode in behind her with his arms folded across his chest.

There was a long, uncomfortable silence as he and his mother just stared at each other.

Adam finally reacted. "Well, uh, I'm going to go—" he pointed toward the door "—to the office and do whatever I can to keep the press at bay until you're ready to make a statement."

His words caused Lucius to look up from his battle of wills with Jocelyn. "Statement?"

Adam nodded from the foyer. "You'll need to say something, Lucius. This is big news. The press will be looking for a sound bite."

"And what do you expect me to say?"

Adam shrugged. "I don't know, you'll figure it out. Ms. Turner." He inclined his head to her and seconds later he was gone, leaving Lucius and his mother alone.

"Oh, joy, what do we do now?" Lucius rubbed his hands together. "Oh, I know. How about you explain why you kept Arthur's identity a secret? Or, I don't know, why don't you tell me why on earth you would *choose* to be that man's mistress for decades? How about we start there?"

"I know you're hurt, Lucius, upset with me about the turn of events, but there's so much you don't know."

Lucius walked over to a nearby chair and sat. "Enlighten me."

"Very well." His mother removed the large hat and placed it and her sunglasses on his glass cocktail table and sat down on his black leather sofa opposite him.

Several beats went by before Lucius said, "I'm waiting."

"May I have a glass of water?" She touched her throat. "I'm feeling a bit parched."

"Ever the drama queen." Lucius rose and returned a couple of minutes later and handed a glass to her. "Let's get on with it, Jocelyn. I don't have all day, because I have to figure out how to fix the mess you've created not only of *your* life, but *mine* as well." He sat down in the seat he'd vacated.

She nodded and took a sip of water. "I met your father at a party after I'd snuck out of Mama's house when I was eighteen years old. Arthur was everything I wasn't. He was twenty-one years old and had just graduated from Stanford. He came from an upper-middle-class family and was going places. We were immediately drawn to each other and embarked on a passionate love affair that summer. Arthur talked to me about his dreams of owning his own business and being his own man outside his father's control."

"Sounds romantic." Lucius snorted, placing his right leg on his opposite thigh.

She ignored the dig and continued. "I thought Arthur was going to marry me because we were head over heels for each other, but later I learned I was wrong. He was already promised to Charlotte Griffin, a beautiful debutante whose father was going to help Arthur get his business off the ground."

"So this boils down to money. He was a greedy bastard who left you pregnant and penniless to marry another woman?"

His mother shook his head. "It wasn't like that, Lucius. I'd planned on telling him I was pregnant with you, but that's the night I found out about Charlotte. I loved him so much that I couldn't stand in the way of his happiness. So I didn't tell him I was pregnant even when your grandma threatened to disown me. And so Arthur married Charlotte and I had you."

Lucius eyes narrowed. "Sounds plausible, but that doesn't explain why you were never around. Why you left me with Grandma Ruby."

"Honestly?"

"That would be appreciated."

"I left you because I couldn't bear to look at you." She turned away from him and sniffed into her handkerchief. "Every time I looked it you, you reminded me of Arthur and the love we'd shared. It was too much. So I took the easy way out."

"That's all fine and good, and maybe it explains your indifference toward your own child. But what about the money? Where did it come from? The boarding school, fancy clothes and vacations. It had to have come from him."

His mother rose from the sofa and walked over to the

French doors of his balcony. She swung them open and sunlight flooded the room—in direct opposition to Lucius's dark mood.

He strode over to her and grasped her shoulders, "I asked you a question, Mother. And I want the truth. *Finally.* I think I deserve that much."

She nodded. "You do. And I'm here to give it to you and endure your wrath."

"My wrath?" Lucius released her. "I just want the T-R-U-T-H. Why is that so hard for you?"

"Because," she shouted. "I loved him. I loved him with all my heart and still do, but I could never *have* him. I was forced to live in the shadows and watch another woman bear his child. Watch him raise another son as his firstborn when it should have been you."

"And whose fault is that, Mother? Yours."

She stepped away from him. "Don't you think I know that? I'm to blame for all of this. I should have told him when the summer ended, but I didn't. And when we reconnected when you were five years old, I couldn't tell him then, either. How could I tell him about the child I'd denied him? Oh, my God!" She let out a long sob. "Instead, I was selfish and rekindled our affair. I allowed him to lavish me with nice things, but I didn't just take it for myself." She turned to Lucius. "I used the money for you, so you could have a better life. But the joke was on me, because you wanted no part of it."

"That's right, Mother. I hated the nannies and boarding schools you put me in because I wasn't with *you*! Don't you get it?" He pointed to his temple. "I just wanted a mother, but you couldn't be bothered."

"I know that. And I felt guilty, so I cut things off with Arthur and tried to move forward with my life. How could I be with him when I was keeping this terrible secret from him? So instead I filled my life up with men and parties as an escape from my past."

"And, well, here we are," Lucius replied. "We've come full circle, Jocelyn. And it's all out there for everyone to see."

"Don't you think I know that? It's been my secret shame."

"So I'm your shame?" Lucius pounded his chest. "Thanks a lot. Now I know how you truly feel."

"No, no." She rushed toward him. "I didn't mean you, Lucius. Never you. I've been ashamed of how I treated you, of how bad a mother I've been to you."

"But you're not ashamed of being his mistress?" Lucius asked, gritting his teeth. "Because clearly you didn't stay away from him."

"No, I didn't," she admitted. "We kept in touch over the years. I suppose we could never fully let each other go. Arthur has never been truly happy with Charlotte even though she bore him a son. And a couple of weeks ago, when I came back here to see you, Arthur asked me to dinner. He was so unhappy and I guess one thing led to another—"

"And you ended up in bed? Again?" Lucius shook his head. Never in a million years could he have dreamed up this story.

"Yes." She lifted her chin, meeting his icy gaze straight on. "It was beautiful and I won't be ashamed, because I love him, and despite all the odds, Arthur still loves me."

Lucius clapped his hand. "What a touching love story you two have. But what about me, Jocelyn? Where do *I* fit in the picture? Do you mean to tell me that he has no idea of my existence?"

Her face clouded with uneasiness, and he noticed her biting her lip as she looked away from his probing eyes. "Well?"

She shook head. "No, he doesn't know."

"That's bull," Lucius snapped. "A man like that had to have known. He had the means to keep track of you and I bet he did for years. *He knew.* And that begs the question as to why he never came forward to meet me, claim me."

"No, he couldn't have known." She shook her head fervently and her face flushed. "If he did, he would have contacted you."

"So naive," Lucius said with contempt. "You—" he pointed to his mother "—I get. I was a constant reminder of a love you could never have. It would be easier to keep me at arm's length. But him? The great Arthur Knight is a coward. He couldn't face me man-to-man and tell me he's my father."

"Don't say that." Jocelyn placed her hands over her ears. "He's a good man."

"He's a rich man that was afraid to lose his fortune if his wife and second son found out my identity. But wouldn't you know, she knew anyway. It was just as easy for her to keep me in the closet, same as him. Because then Charlotte Knight got to stay in the lifestyle she'd grown accustomed to as lady of the manor. It's all coming to me now. It was a win-win for all you while Max and I are in the dark."

"Max?"

"My brother," Lucius responded. "I saw him last night. Saw the devastation on his face to learn he had a brother he knew nothing about and the lies and deceit our parents have lived with for decades."

He strode toward the door and held it open. "Get out!"

"Lucius…"

"I heard what you had to say and now I want you to leave."

"But—"

"Go, Jocelyn. Haven't you done enough? You denied me

my birthright, the father I've longed for my entire life, refusing to tell me time and time again when I pleaded with you. And now I find out he's been right under my nose the entire time?" He laughed contemptuously. "I don't want anything to do with either of you, ever again. I'm tired of the lies. It's time I start living the truth, *my* truth."

She grasped her hat, sunglasses and purse and headed for the door. "What does that mean, Lucius?"

"I guess you're just going to have to wait and see like everyone else." And he closed the door behind her.

Chapter 17

Naomi couldn't believe it had been two days since she'd heard from Lucius. He'd sneaked out of her house like a thief in the middle of the night, stealing her heart along with him. Why, oh, why had she been so foolish as to let her feelings slip from her lips? He had to have heard her whisper she loved him. That's why he stayed away.

Lucius didn't do commitment. She'd known that from the start. He was a love 'em and leave 'em playboy. And she'd just been left.

It hurt knowing that he didn't feel the same way about her. She'd given him all of herself, and she'd thought that his coming to her after hearing such devastating news was his way of opening up to her, letting her in.

She'd been wrong.

Instead, she got silence. Her calls, texts and emails went unanswered. At first she thought he was just avoiding her, but then his assistant had finally taken pity on her and told her he hadn't been into the office in days.

The savvy media had put two and two together and realized that Lucius Knight was indeed Arthur's illegitimate son. There was much speculation in the local paper about what that would mean for Maximus Xavier Knight, heir apparent to Knight Shipping. Would he have to share his inheritance if his father died?

Arthur Knight was hanging on, but the prognosis wasn't good, probably because the man couldn't get any peace worrying about his entire life turning on its ear. Not that Naomi could feel sorry for him. He had to have known Lucius existed and had done nothing about it. Never acknowledging he was Lucius's father was a pretty heartless thing to do.

Despite how much she hurt for Lucius, life had to go on. Naomi would soon find herself out of a job if Lucius bought Kelsey's 25.5 percent. It would make him majority shareholder.

Naomi wasn't ready for that, and she most certainly wasn't ready to have to work with him every day. It would be a reminder that he didn't love her, and that she couldn't abide.

She needed to talk this out, so she called Kelsey, who was at a park near her home. Apparently, she'd been going stir-crazy in the house with Bella and had told Owen she had to take her out so she could run off some excess energy.

Naomi found Kelsey seated on a park bench watching Bella play on the slide. "Hey, Kels." She smiled when she saw her pregnant friend's very large belly.

"Wow! Have you blown up overnight." Naomi couldn't resist speaking her thoughts aloud.

Kelsey's brows pulled together. "Thanks a lot, Naomi. Don't you know you're not supposed to criticize a pregnant woman's weight? We're very sensitive."

"Oh, please, heifer," Naomi laughed, "you have much too much confidence. Plus, you're all belly anyway."

Kelsey's cheeks were a touch round, but her biceps and legs were exactly the same.

"That's because I was working out up until Caden—" she rubbed her belly "—decided to give us a scare."

"You look fantastic and you know it."

"Two months to go."

Naomi smiled. "That's right, you have to keep that bun in the oven. So no stress, all right?" She pointed her finger at her.

"I'm not stressed." Kelsey glanced at the slide her daughter was playing around. "Bella, stay where I can see you!"

The blue-eyed blonde with the gorgeous ringlets was the spitting image of her mother and quickly complied thanks to the stern tone of Kelsey's voice.

Kelsey turned to her. "I'd be a lot less anxious if Adam would return my or my husband's calls. I thought he wanted our shares."

"You've heard the news?"

"That Lucius could be Arthur Knight's son?" Kelsey inquired. "Yes, and it was pretty shocking. How's he dealing with it?"

Naomi shrugged. "Wouldn't know. I haven't seen or heard from him since the night he found out. He's MIA."

"Oh, Naomi." Kelsey reached across the short distance between them to pat her hand. "I'm sorry, honey. I told you to be careful about falling for that man."

"Too late." Tears formed in Naomi's eyes, "I already did. I'm in love with him, Kelsey, but he doesn't want me."

"You can't save him, Naomi," Kelsey said. "He's always been a loner. It's the only way he knows how to be. Perhaps he doesn't know what it's like to have love in his life."

"That—" Naomi pointed her index finger "—that I could understand if he talked to me. Then we could maybe work through it, but he's shut me out. He'd prefer to deal with this on his own."

"I'm sure it's hard to break old habits, Naomi. Here's a man who has never had a father, never known the kind of love that you and I have. He could be struggling to make sense of things. Maybe you can give him a little slack until he comes to grips with the situation."

Naomi stared back at Kelsey, stunned. "Where is all this compassion coming from? I thought you didn't like Lucius."

"I've never disliked Lucius," Kelsey replied. "I've just always been worried that you might love him more than he loves you. I worry that you're more invested, because when you love, you love deeply and with your whole heart. And—and—" her voice broke as she fought back tears "—I just want you to find someone who's worthy of that love, Naomi."

"Aw, Kelsey." Naomi leaned in for a hug, but she didn't make it very far with Kelsey's belly between them.

They both laughed. "I can't even hug you right." Kelsey chuckled. "I really have become big overnight."

"Big and beautiful," Naomi said with a genuine smile. She would try to remember Kelsey's words. Perhaps she was right. Maybe all Lucius needed was time to come to terms with his parentage in his own way. Naomi would give him all the time he needed. She just hoped that when he was ready, he would come back to her.

Dead. Arthur Knight was dead. Stunned, Lucius ended the call on his cell phone and sat back on the sofa in his living room. He'd suffered a second heart attack in the hospital and they'd been unable to revive him.

He'd only just found out he had a father three days ago.

He'd been trying to come to terms with the lot he'd been dealt in life, only to have Arthur suddenly ripped away.

It wasn't right.

It wasn't fair.

How could this have happened? Why hadn't he gone to him and tried to make some sort of peace when he had the chance? Instead, he'd wasted time and now it was too late. He was gone.

Lucius would never know the truth. Were his suspicions right? Had Arthur known about him? How had he felt about Lucius? Lucius would never have the answers he so desperately needed.

His mother was partially to blame for this travesty. She'd kept the truth from him when he could have had years getting to know the man. They might not have had a normal father-son relationship, but at least they would have had something.

Instead, all he was left with was regret. Although, he'd only known of Arthur's existence for a short time, he could have pushed past that she devil of a wife of his and made his presence known. Instead, he'd reverted back to his teenage years, sullen and withdrawn. It came easy to him, because it was his comfort zone. Heaven forbid he would ever do the unexpected.

He bet the Knights had counted on that, counted on his cowardice, and he'd proven them right.

Lucius needed to escape. Flee from the present. Run from the past and drown in his sorrows. And he knew just the place to go to make him forget.

"Tim, what are you doing here?" Naomi asked when her brother stopped by to visit her at work two days later. He was dressed in his usual office attire of trousers and a collared shirt as he approached her desk.

She'd just finished listening to a pitch on some new products they were considering. They were all great ideas, but Naomi hesitated debuting any of them while she was unsure of her place in the company. Once Lucius purchased the lion's share of Brooks and Johnson stock, he would have enough leverage to convince the board to replace her, the founding partner, if he wanted to.

Not that she knew what was going on with Lucius. She'd seen reports that Arthur Knight had died on Wednesday. She'd been heartbroken for him, knowing now he would never get a chance to get to know the man with whom he shared a bloodline. Naomi had again reached out to him, calling repeatedly, but nothing.

Lucius didn't want to be found, and he sure as hell didn't want to talk to her.

Tim frowned, and Naomi became uneasy. She'd never seen this look on his face before, a mixture of sadness with a tinge of relief. "What's going on?"

"You haven't heard?"

"Heard what? I've been in a closed-door session all morning," Naomi responded, rising from her chair and walking toward him.

"Then it's good I got here first." Tim reached for her hand. "Come sit with me."

"Why?" Naomi asked as he led her to the sofa in her sitting area. "Tim, you're scaring me."

"I'm sorry. I don't mean to do that, but I thought you might need me after you see this." He pulled a newspaper from behind his back and showed her the front page.

Naomi stared in horror at the headline: Playboy vs. Heir Apparent—Who Will Win? But that wasn't the worst offense. There, in color for the entire community to see, was Lucius, cuddled up with an unidentified half-dressed female who was darn near sitting in his lap.

Naomi turned her head away. "I don't want to see that."

Tim tossed the tabloid in the trash can nearest to him. "Better you see it now and know who you're dealing with, Naomi. During lunch, when I saw everyone reading it, I knew I had to get to you."

"Why? To show me what a fool I've been for thinking that Lucius actually cared for me?" Naomi laughed derisively.

"No." Tim reached for her and pulled her into his embrace. "Because I know how much you care for him. That night when you brought him over to meet the family, I could see how besotted you were with the man. The same way you'd been when you were fifteen. And I knew this would hurt."

"It does." Naomi nodded against the comfort of her brother's chest. She wanted to cry, but instead all she felt was anger. "It helps me see how stupid I've been to think I matter to Lucius."

"You're not stupid, Naomi." Tim took her chin between his thumb and forefinger and forced her to look up at him. "You're trusting and open. And it made you susceptible, given your former feelings for this man. He took advantage of that, and instead of appreciating the woman he had in front of him, he looked elsewhere."

Naomi blinked back tears that threatened to fall. "True, but I knew who he was, Tim. He never said he was going to change or offered me anything more than living in the moment. I was the one who was foolish to think we'd shared something special. Now I see I was wrong. Lucius has moved on."

She stood up.

"What are you going to do?" Tim asked as he rose.

"I'm going to move on, same as him." Naomi knew saying the words were easier said than done. She was putting on a brave front with Tim because she didn't want him to see how truly devastated she was. She wanted to fall apart in private.

Tim caressed her arm. "All right, kid." He pulled her into one last hug and kissed the top of her head. "Call me if you need *anything*."

Naomi breathed in heavily, holding on to her sorrow. "Will do." She glanced up at Tim and gave him a brief smile as he left her office.

Only once he'd gone did she clutch her hand to her mouth and release the sob she'd been holding inside.

"Well, well, well, I finally found you," Adam said the next afternoon when on a whim he decided to check the gentleman's club he and Lucius liked to frequent. "I've been looking for you everywhere."

Lucius didn't look up as he stared into his nearly empty scotch glass. He'd been at the club for nearly forty-eight hours drinking away his troubles. The barkeep hadn't seemed to mind, because he knew it would be one helluva bill given Lucius only drank top-shelf liquor. He'd also ensured Lucius hadn't lacked for company, and several women—including one waitress who'd been his favorite bedmate in the past—had been his companions for the entire evening.

She knew the right words to say to stroke his ego, and they'd sat in a corner booth, drinking and smoking stogies for much of the night. However, when she'd suggested a private room upstairs, Lucius had declined. As beautiful as she was, he wasn't interested. There was only one woman that lit his fire. Naomi.

Adam snapped his fingers in front of Lucius's face. "Are you listening to me?"

Lucius greeted him with an icy stare. "Perhaps I didn't want to be found. Did you ever think of that?"

"Yeah, I did," Adam replied, "because you've always been a sulker, even when we were teenagers, but I thought I'd weaned you off that habit."

His good-natured response caused Lucius to glance up, and a slight smile creased the corners of his mouth.

"See, I can still make you laugh," Adam said with a grin.

"Yeah, well, I don't have a lot to laugh about these days."

"That's bull, Lucius. I'm not going to give in to your pity party." He tried snatching the glass away, but Lucius held on to it with a death grip.

"Don't mess with my drink."

"I know you're angry, man. Hurt, even, and I'm truly sorry Arthur passed away before you ever got a chance to know him, but that's life, Lucius. Sometimes bad things happen. So what you didn't get to have a daddy? You grew up just fine without one. You had your grandma Ruby, who has loved you unconditionally from the jump. And look at what you've been able to accomplish—I bet the old man secretly admired all you were able to do without him in your life. You used your past to inspire you to greatness. Not many men can say the same. So what Arthur Knight didn't acknowledge you as his son. You're a wealthy man in your own right. It should taste all the more sweet."

Lucius didn't like hearing what Adam had to say, even though he knew there was some truth to his words. He needed time to think about his next move, to get his footing and figure out his place now that he was part of the Knight family and all that would entail. "I don't need or want your pep talk, Adam. Can't you just leave me in peace to drink?"

"I could, but we have business to attend to. If you want to position yourself to be the majority shareholder of Brooks and Johnson, you have to act now and lock in Kelsey's stock before she sells it to someone else."

"If that's what you're here to pester me about, just do it," Lucius said. He motioned to the bartender to refill his drink.

"Are you sure about this?" Adam asked leaning against the bar stool. "You don't want to talk to Naomi first?"

"Naomi?" Even saying her name caused an ache in his belly, but he couldn't deal with that part of his life right now. He was too deep in his own misery to take someone else's feelings into account.

"Yeah, the woman you've been hitting the sheets with for weeks," Adam responded. "And the very same woman who is ready to read you the riot act for this." Adam threw down a tabloid.

"What's this?" Lucius snatched up a local tabloid magazine and saw the headline, Playboy vs. Heir Apparent—Who Will Win? There was a picture of Lucius slouched in a booth with a cigar in one hand and the waitress from last night in his lap, along with another picture of Maximus Knight, looking debonair in a business suit, standing in front of the Knight Shipping compound. "What the hell?" He turned to Adam. "When did this come out?"

"This morning. It's one—though not the only—reason I wanted to reach you. The press is really going to play you against your brother over who will run Knight Shipping."

"I couldn't care less about Knight Shipping."

"You should. You could be entitled to a share of it."

"I care about Naomi. If she saw this—" he pointed to the paper on the bar "—she'll think…" He couldn't say the words aloud. She'd think he'd been with another woman after she'd been there for him. Comforted him. Made love to him. Loved him. "I have to go. Can you take care of the bill?" Lucius jumped off the bar stool and started toward the door.

Adam nodded. "Sure thing. And the shares of Brooks and Johnson?"

"I'll take care of it." Lucius waved him off as he rushed out the door and to Naomi's.

Chapter 18

When Lucius arrived home to shower and change before he went to Naomi's, the press was everywhere. He found his penthouse swarming with reporters, cameramen and television trucks. He barely made it into his garage through the throng. On his way out, he'd have to be stealthy if he didn't want them following him to his intended destination.

After a shave and an overdue long, hot shower to clear his head, Lucius dressed in trousers and a dress shirt sans tie. He hoped Naomi would believe him. Although he hadn't clearly defined his feelings for her, he didn't want her to think he was callous enough to jump from her bed into another woman's with no regard for her feelings. He wished he could offer her more than that, but he was confused. The last several days had been a whirlwind for him. He hadn't been prepared for the flood of emotions that had enveloped him upon learning his heritage only to have it so violently taken away from him.

Arthur's death had set him down a dangerous path. If Adam hadn't gotten to him, he would have gone farther into the rabbit hole. Then there was his mother. Jocelyn wasn't letting up on calling him, and she'd recruited his grandmother. He didn't want his grandma upset and planned on going to see her after he'd cleared the air with Naomi.

Lucius arranged with the apartment complex for one of the bellmen to take his place in the vehicle he'd arrived in, while Lucius would take a different car. His plan worked out perfectly. When he pulled out of his garage in his Porsche, the press had disappeared, having followed the bellman in his Bentley. He was free and clear.

As he drove, Lucius reflected on what he was going to say Naomi. If she'd seen the tabloids, he would apologize and tell her that the press got it all wrong. He hoped that it would alleviate any qualms she might have, but deep down Lucius wondered exactly what Naomi's reaction would be when he showed up to her door unannounced.

Naomi swung open the door and was surprised to find Lucius on her doorstep, given he'd systematically ignored her for the last five days, since he'd sneaked out of her bed. She didn't speak to him; instead she closed the door in his face and walked away.

"Naomi, wait!" Lucius caught the door before it shut and entered her bungalow.

She turned around and gave him a hostile glare. "Did I ask you in?"

"No," he began, but she interrupted him.

"Then perhaps you should leave," Naomi replied. "Because there's nothing for you here. That is, unless you want to hit it one more time for the road before you go back to being the playboy."

"I suppose I deserve that for how I left you the other night," Lucius responded. "But I'd like to talk to you." He reached for her arm.

"Don't touch me!" Naomi snatched her arm away. "Don't you dare touch me!"

Lucius held up his hands in the air. "All right, all right. I won't touch you, but we have some unfinished business."

"Ha." Naomi snorted and padded over to her couch. She sat down with her legs folded underneath her. She didn't bother looking to see if he was following, because she knew he was. He'd come to say his peace, and although she wouldn't believe a word that came out of his mouth, she'd listen.

Lucius joined her in the living room, but rather than sit beside her, he wisely chose the adjacent chair. He leaned down and faced her with his arms resting on his thighs. He let out a long sigh as if pondering his words. She noticed him glance at her coffee table to see the tabloid and the picture of him with the other woman across the front page. She'd retrieved it from the trash in her office as a reminder to never be stupid again where Lucius Knight was concerned.

"Well?"

His dark eyes glanced up and focused on hers, and Naomi felt the familiar tug whenever she was around him. She was angry that he could still make her feel lust for him when she knew he wasn't interested in anything other than sex from her.

"You saw the tabloid?"

She didn't answer, she just glared at him. She'd think that much was obvious.

"And I suppose you think that I've been using you this entire time and couldn't wait to get back to my former lifestyle?" Lucius surmised.

Still she remained silent.

"It's not like that, Naomi. That picture doesn't show the depth of despair and turmoil I've been going through since learning Arthur was my father. And I admit I could have handled it better."

"You mean sexing me in my own house and running out like a thief in the night?" Naomi responded.

Lucius visibly winced. "I'm sorry I made you feel like that, Naomi. That wasn't my intent. That night I needed you and you were there for me, and I'm grateful that you were. And I'm sorry that I didn't call you to let you know I was okay, but it was bit much to take in all at once. And Arthur's death has only added to it."

"Don't you think I know that, Lucius?" Naomi folded her arms across her chest. "I wanted to be there for you, but you shut me out."

"I—I recognize that." He spoke slowly, as if he were choosing his words very carefully. "But I needed to handle this alone and in my own way."

"Oh, you weren't alone," Naomi replied, pointing to the tabloid. "You've had several females to keep your bed warm."

Lucius glanced down at the paper and back at her. "I—I'm sure it looks that way, but that wasn't the case."

"What I do know, Lucius," Naomi replied quickly, "is that I never should have trusted you. You're the same player you've always been, bedding women and then tossing them aside when you're done with them. Silly me, I thought I was different—" she laughed scornfully "—but the joke is on me." She rose from the sofa. "I've heard what you had to say and now you can leave."

She started toward the foyer.

"Naomi!" Lucius rose to his full six-foot-two height and blocked her path. "Don't do this. I don't want to leave like this."

"Like what, Lucius?" She glanced up at him. His dark eyes were unfathomable—she couldn't read him any more than she ever could, except maybe when they were filled with lust. "You and I both know this—" she motioned back and forth between them "—was never going anyplace, right? You only wanted Brooks and Johnson, and in the process I caught your eye and you decided you wanted to have sex with me."

Naomi shrugged. "I get it. I really do. Well, you've done both. You took me to bed and Kelsey's ready to sell you her shares. You won! I've nothing left to give you, Lucius. And you sure as hell have nothing to give me."

"Naomi, please." Lucius's arm circled around her waist.

Naomi hated that her traitorous body trembled at his touch. A riot of sensation coursed through her system. That he could still have an effect on her even though she knew he didn't truly care about her. He didn't love her like she loved him.

"Stop!" Naomi pushed at the hard wall of his chest, trying to get distance from him.

"Baby…" He tried to pull her into his embrace, but she pushed him again.

"Stop! Don't *baby* me, Lucius," she cried out. "I told you I loved you. The last time we were together. I admitted how I felt about you. And yet here you stand, not even acknowledging those feelings."

Lucius stared at her. She was right. He'd thought she might be too preoccupied with the tabloid to bring up her declaration of love, but he was wrong. Naomi was a strong woman and she wasn't backing down.

"Nothing to say, slick?" Naomi jeered, calling him by the nickname she'd given him that he disliked. "Cat got your tongue?"

He was torn. He didn't want to hurt her, yet he wasn't ready to say the words it was so clear she needed to hear back. Even though he'd felt the emotion. At times when they were together, Lucius had wondered if he was indeed falling in love with Naomi, but loving someone who had the power to hurt him scared him.

Naomi stared at him wide-eyed, waiting for his response.

"I—I…" He stumbled over his words. It was the first time in his life he was ever unsure of himself, of what to say. He couldn't tell her what she needed to hear, but he could show her.

So he acted instead. He reached for her, pulling her firm against him and then dipped his head. Her lips parted beneath his. He didn't know if her response was because he'd surprised her or because she was submitting to him, but he enjoyed it all the same. He delved into her mouth, gliding his tongue back and forth across hers until he heard her moan. He backed her up, pinning her between the wall and him as he ravaged her mouth.

His blood felt like liquid fire in his veins, and his body pulsed with the need to bury himself inside her. He needed this. It had been days since he'd tasted her. And she tasted the same. No, better than he remembered. Naomi was an unforgettable woman, and the all-consuming passion he felt with her was like nothing else he'd ever known. There was no way he could look at, let alone *be* with another woman. So why couldn't he tell her he loved her?

His fingers began creeping beneath her top, and the jolt of reality must have hit her in the face, because Naomi sprang away from him as if she'd been burned.

Naomi gulped in a breath. "Okay, you've proven that I'm still weak for you, that I have no self-control, but I do have some modicum of self-respect. And I want more, Lucius, but you're just not capable of giving me what I want—what I need. So you have to go."

He stared at her for several long beats. He wanted to wrap her in his arms and take her to her bedroom and remind her how good they were together. But what would that solve?

"Please go, Lucius," she ordered when he hadn't made a move to leave.

"All right, I'll go." Lucius walked to the door and opened it but turned to glance back at her. "But I need you to know that it wasn't just sex for me, Naomi. I do care for you. Perhaps not in the way you need me to right now, but I do care."

He closed the door behind him and quietly walked to the car. Once inside, he glanced back at the craftsman-style house. He knew Naomi was crying inside. He wanted to go in and comfort her, to tell her he loved her, but he couldn't.

So he drove away.

"Lucius, I'm so glad you came to see me," his grandmother said when he stopped by her home later that evening.

He'd had to take some time to get himself together before he dropped by. His visit at Naomi's had been the hardest thing he'd ever had to do. To see her hurting and to be unable to fix it was heart-wrenching and had shaken him to the core. He'd thought about going back to the gentleman's club and drowning his sorrows again, but what would that do?

Instead, he'd stopped by the office to go through the hundreds of emails and calls he'd received while he'd been MIA the last several days. It was there that he'd seen an envelope from a courier sitting on his desk.

When he'd opened it, he'd been shocked to see it was from an attorney's office. After tearing it open, he'd scanned the letter and tossed it down. Inside was his invitation to the reading of Arthur Knight's will. What the hell? The man had never even acknowledged his existence and now all of sudden he'd been invited to the reading of his will? Why? What did it mean? And would he go?

If nothing else, he should to satisfy his curiosity as to what Arthur could possibly have wanted to say in death that he hadn't been able to say in Lucius's thirty-four years of life.

He brought the letter with him to his grandmother's, because if anyone could help him make sense of it all, it was her. He was, however, shocked to see she had a guest when he walked into the living room. "Mother." He regarded Jocelyn quizzically as he sat down. "What's going on, Grandma?"

She followed him into the room. "I figured someone had to get you two together to talk."

"That's not your place, Grandma."

"Like hell, it isn't, boy," she responded hotly and pounded her chest. "I raised you, because she was too afraid to face you. Too afraid to stay and be the mother she should have been. Too afraid to tell you about your father, and now he's gone."

"That's right, Grandma. And it's because of her that I never got to know the man. And he's dead. D-E-A-D." Lucius glared at his mother, whose eyes glistened with unshed tears.

"I know I'm to blame, Lucius," Jocelyn said. "I—I just thought I was doing what was best for you, what was best for everybody."

"By taking away my choices?" Lucius asked. "And leaving me fatherless? Motherless?"

His mother lowered her head. "I'm so sorry, you don't know how much. Sometimes, Mama—" she looked up at her mother "—I think about how different things would have been if I'd told Arthur I was pregnant with Lucius." She shook her head in frustration. "But I didn't. And—and I can't take it back. Instead I'm left out in the cold to grieve for him alone. I can't even go the funeral."

"You're here because of your choices, Jocelyn," Ruby responded. "There's no denying that, but—"

Lucius interrupted her. "She doesn't have the monopoly on grief, Grandma. I didn't get invited, either. Instead all I got is this." He held up the envelope. "An invitation to the reading of the will."

"That's something, Lucius. Perhaps he'll acknowledge you in some way," Jocelyn said hopefully, sitting up straight.

"Because he was too cowardly to do it in person?" Lucius snorted.

"I didn't bring you both here to gripe at each other." His grandmother stepped between them. "I brought you here because you both—" she looked in Lucius's direction "—are grieving. I think you could lean on each other during this time, help each other through it."

Lucius shook his head. "I'm sorry, Grandma, but that's never going to happen. I will never forgive her for denying me my father. Never."

He rose to leave, but his grandmother stopped him. "All this anger you have inside you, Lucius. It isn't good. You have to let it go. You have to forgive. If you don't, it'll eat you alive and taint everything that's good in your life—like that young lady you're in love with."

His mother perked up from her seat. "What young lady?"

Lucius turned to glare at her. "That's no concern of yours."

"Lucius," his grandmother reprimanded.

"Her name's Naomi Brooks. But it doesn't matter anyway. Naomi wants nothing to do with me. Why? Because I have a block of ice where my heart should be," Lucius responded. "And that's because of you." He looked in his mother's direction.

"Baby." His grandmother moved from her chair and cupped both his cheeks in her small, frail hands. "Don't you see? It doesn't have to be. You don't have to be alone anymore. If this girl loves you as much as I suspect she does, then all you have to do is open your heart and allow the love in. Tell her how you feel. I promise you, love will help heal your heart like no other."

"Grandma…"

"Trust me, boy, I've been on this earth a lot longer than you. Tell her you love her 'cause I know you do. I see it." She motioned with her two forefingers between both their eyes. "I saw it the first time you told me about her, but you've been too scared or too blind to see it."

"Mama's right." His mother rose from her seat. "Don't be like me. Don't let love slip through your fingers, Lucius. Otherwise, you'll regret it forever."

Were they right? Lucius thought. Was it possible to have the love he'd always wanted in his life if he just reached out and grabbed it? If he told Naomi he loved her, would she accept him with all his flaws and baggage? Would she be with him always? There was only one way to find out.

Chapter 19

"I had the papers drawn up as you requested," Adam said, sliding the stack across Lucius's desk and stepping back.

"Thank you," Lucius said, looking up from his computer monitor.

"Are you sure you don't want me to take care of this for you?" Adam inquired. "I know you have a lot on your plate."

"No, I want to do it," Lucius replied.

"All right. You know once you do this, you'll own majority interest in Brooks and Johnson."

"I'm aware."

"You know Naomi won't be happy about this. You're going to get a lot of resistance from her on any changes you want to implement."

"I can handle Naomi."

"Famous last words," Adam laughed. "Any man that thinks he can handle a woman has grossly underestimated her. She could cause you real headaches if you're not careful."

Since he'd left his grandmother's nearly a week ago, he'd given serious thought to what she'd said. And had come to a conclusion on what he had to do next. When all was said and done.

"You might be right about that." Lucius closed the folder he'd been working on. "Which is why I'm putting a plan in motion that will ensure I have Naomi on my side."

"That sounds mysterious," Adam replied. "Care to explain?"

Lucius shook his head. "Nope. But you'll see soon enough." He rose from his chair, grabbed the envelope with the papers Adam had drawn up and headed toward the door without another word.

"Daddy, what are you doing here?" Naomi asked when her father found her sitting on her favorite love seat in her parents' backyard, wrapped in a blanket.

"C'mon, baby girl," he said, joining her on the love seat and underneath the blanket. "I know where you go when you have something on your mind. You want to go someplace peaceful, quiet, so you can allow yourself to be introspective. Same as me. Plus, Gemma called and said your car was parked outside the house in the middle of the day."

Naomi smiled. Her sister was always a little too nosy for her own good. Couldn't she start her weekend early if she wanted to? "Yes, I guess I got that gene from you." She bumped her shoulder with his.

"You've always been the most like me," he said. "Tim is like your mother. He's more deliberate, but you and me, we're all heart. Always have been and always will be."

"Yeah, well, wearing my heart on my sleeve has gotten me in the predicament I'm in."

"And what's that?"

"In love with a man who doesn't love me back."

"Lucius."

Naomi nodded. She'd hoped that Kelsey had been right

and that Lucius perhaps was too overwrought or caught up in his emotions to tell her he loved her, but it had been nearly a week since she'd kicked him out of her house and she hadn't heard from him. It had hurt more, because she'd gotten her hopes up that Kelsey had been on to something, but she too had been wrong. Lucius didn't care about Naomi any more than he did the hundreds of other women he'd been with.

Apparently she wasn't so special, even though he *cared* for her.

"I don't believe that," her father said. "Did he say that?"

She turned to him. "No, but it was what he didn't say that made it crystal clear how he feels about me, Daddy."

"Then he's a fool if he doesn't realize what a gem he has in you."

Naomi smiled. "Daddy…"

He circled his arm around her shoulders and gave them a gentle squeeze. "I love you, baby girl. And one day you'll find someone worthy of all the love you have in your heart."

"I know. I just wanted Lucius to be that man."

"I know, pumpkin." He cupped her head to his shoulder. "Just give it some time. Because in time, it'll hurt a little less."

Naomi doubted that was even possible. Lucius was her first love, and she wasn't sure she'd ever find another man that made her feel like he did. He made her feel sexy and alive, bold and daring, as if she could do anything when she was with him. She missed that feeling. Would she ever find it again?

"Lucius, this is a risky move." Kelsey handed Lucius back the pen after she'd signed her shares of Brooks and Johnson over to him later that afternoon.

After receiving the papers from Adam, Lucius had come directly from the office to Kelsey's home in Belmont Shore. He'd known he would have to act quickly, not just for his sake, but before they sold to another buyer. Adam had gotten wind that another of his competitors had made the Johnsons an offer.

"Yes, I know."

"Naomi was on the fence on whether she wanted me to sell to you," Kelsey responded, rubbing her seven-months-pregnant belly. "Owen and I were seriously entertaining another offer to make Naomi's life as easy as possible during this transition."

"Yes, I'd heard about the other group, which is why I had to move."

"But if what you've told me is true and your intentions are honorable, this could end beautifully." Kelsey smiled. "And I want that for my best friend. No, my sister, because Naomi is that important to me."

"I know that, Kelsey," Lucius said. "And I promise you, I won't let you down. I won't betray the trust you have in me. And I will be good to Naomi and good for her."

Kelsey pointed her finger at him. "You'd better. Because if you hurt her, I will come after you after I have this baby."

Lucius laughed as he imagined Kelsey holding a baby in one arm and a toddler in another, chasing him down the street with a bat. "I don't doubt you would, Kelsey, but I have the best intentions." He used his index finger to make a cross over his heart. "Scout's honor."

Now all he had to do over the weekend was get all the pieces in place.

As she drove in to work on Monday morning, Naomi was ready for whatever the day had in store. The talk with her father on Friday had helped. It always did. He had a way of calming her like no one else could. Over the weekend, she'd had time to reflect and realized she would have to face her feelings for Lucius head-on. He'd own a significant share of her company when he purchased Kelsey's stock, and there would be no way around it.

She didn't know how much of a role he wanted to play at Brooks and Johnson and if she'd have to see him every day, but somehow, someway, she would be strong. She wouldn't let him see how much she hurt inside because he didn't share her love. It would take a long time for her to get over him, but she'd done it once before when she'd been a teenager, except this time was different. This wasn't the crush of a young girl longing to date and heal the hot loner bad boy.

She was a grown woman now. And she'd experienced pure bliss in Lucius's arms. With the few lovers she'd had in the past, she'd never felt the way he made her feel. When she was with Lucius, the need and desire to be together was so strong, so potent, she thought she'd die if he didn't touch her again. And when they were just having fun and being normal, it was awesome. But it was over between them, and she would have to go on without being able to kiss him, touch him, make love to him.

Naomi pulled her Audi into the parking space outside her building. She said her hellos and morning greetings to her staff as she made her way to the elevator. She pressed the up button for the top floor and anxiously tapped her foot against the tile. When the doors opened, Naomi stepped out and made her way down the carpeted hallway to her corner office.

"Naomi." Sophie was waiting for her in the hallway and blocking her path.

"Good morning." Naomi was surprised to see her. She

tried stepping around her, but Sophie took the same two steps, blocking her path.

"Good morning, Naomi," she said, rather loudly in Naomi's opinion.

Naomi stared at her strangely. "Are you okay, Sophie? You're acting weird this morning."

Sophie glanced behind her at Naomi's door. "Oh, I—I'm fine. I'm just so happy to see you," she said again, very loudly.

Naomi smiled. She was glad that she had the kind of relationship with her employees that boasted mutual respect and admiration. "It's good to see you, too. Now, if you don't mind—" She stepped around her swiftly and reached for her door handle. "Hold all my calls, I have to catch up on a few things this morning."

"With pleasure," Sophie said excitedly as Naomi pulled the door lever.

When she opened her door, Naomi was shocked to see hundreds of roses in every shade and color sprinkled throughout her office. The scent was overwhelming, but nothing was more so than seeing Lucius standing in the middle of her office in a silver designer suit with a black tie and a large grin spread across his full lips.

"Lucius?" Naomi was taken aback and stood at the doorway, ready to flee. "Wh-what are you doing here?"

"Isn't it obvious?" he asked, coming toward her with his arms stretched out. "I've come to win you back."

When he reached her, he pulled her inside, enveloping her in his arms. Naomi breathed in the spicy, woodsy scent of his cologne that she loved so much. It was all Lucius. A Lucius she loved with all her heart, but she mustn't get carried away by such a grand gesture. She had to hear him out, find out why he was here.

Reluctantly, she pulled away and looked up at him. "I don't understand."

"Come." He took her hand in his large one and led her over to the sofa. He didn't let go of her hand; instead he followed her movements as she sat down on the edge of the sofa, unsure just how long this conversation would last.

"Naomi," Lucius began. "I'm sorry about last week. How I left things between us."

The memory of the pain of his rejection of her and her love still stung, and she slid her hand out of his. "There's nothing to be sorry about. You don't feel the same way about me, and I'll just have to accept that."

He shook his head. "That's not true, Naomi."

She stared at him, perplexed.

"From the moment you came back into my life, I've known you were someone special. No—" he stopped himself "—I think I knew before, when we were in high school, when you were this awkward teenager with bad acne and hair, who wore baggy clothes and followed me around. I knew then that I liked you. You were different from all the other girls who were just interested in me for my looks or because they wanted to show off to their friends that they were hanging with the bad boy."

"I sensed that you were hurting," Naomi stated.

"I know. And you wanted to be a friend and perhaps more, but I was too blind to see it back then. All I could think about back then was blocking out the pain. And since then I've been doing the same thing. Using sex as a crutch as a way to keep women at arm's length, but what I've come to realize is that all those other girls were just fill-ins for you."

Naomi's heart turned over in her chest at Lucius's words, and tears welled in her eyes. With the pad of his thumb, he wiped an errant tear from her cheek.

"You may not believe this, and I don't think I knew it myself, but I'd been waiting for you my entire life, Naomi. And somehow, despite all the odds, fate brought us back together. When I first learned about your IPO last year and started buying shares, I didn't know why I was drawn to you, to your story. It must have been my gut telling me that it was time I finally acted on those feelings I had for you long ago. When I searched you out in Anaheim, I told myself it was to convince you to sell to me, but deep down I knew better. Deep down I knew it was because I wanted you."

"You did?"

He nodded. "And when we reconnected, I sensed that you were as attracted to me as I was to you. I was overjoyed, and I admit I used my charm to break down your defenses. But imagine my surprise when I discovered heaven in your arms."

The breath caught in Naomi's throat and she didn't know if she could let it out. Could this really be happening? Could Lucius really be pouring out his soul to her?

Lucius could see the shock in Naomi's eyes as he laid his soul bare. He'd thought it would be easy, and he'd tried practicing the speech he'd give and how he'd tell her he loved her. Instead, he was rambling on about the past, but somehow he would get the words out. He would say the three words she longed to hear and that he couldn't wait to say aloud.

"I feel the same way," Naomi said. "Being with you was everything." She touched his cheek with the palm of her hand.

He took her hand in his and bent over it. He pressed his lips against her hot skin. Lucius had never felt this way, this level of intensity with any woman.

"I'm sorry if I ever made you feel this was just about sex for me, because it wasn't."

Naomi nodded. "I know, because you *care* for me."

There it was. The line she'd always remember. He cared for her. Not loved her. Cared for her. He hated that she did and vowed to erase it from her memory. He looked into her eyes, searching for—what? That somehow her love had suddenly vanished? It hadn't. He saw a glittering in her eyes, the sentiment he'd always seen. Love.

"I more than care for you, baby. I love you, Naomi."

"You do?" The hopefulness in her voice stole his heart.

He nodded. "I do. I love you. I think I have for some time, but I was just too afraid to see it, to admit it. When you told me how you felt, I wanted to run in the other direction."

"Why?"

"Because I've never felt worthy or deserving of love. My mother left me and my father never claimed me. If it wasn't for my grandmother, I would have been all alone."

"Oh, Lucius." Naomi threw her hands around his neck and pulled him into her embrace. She clutched him to her chest, and Lucius hugged her back tightly. He could feel his throat constricting, tightening, yet he felt like his heart was expanding at the same time. He hadn't thought it was possible that he'd ever feel love in his life.

Naomi pulled away slightly to cup both his cheeks in her hands. "I love you, too, Lucius. I never stopped. And I'll always love you."

She leaned in slightly, tilted her head and then kissed him. Lucius kissed her back with all the love, pent-up desire and passion he'd been holding in all week. He enjoyed the velvety slide of her tongue, the warmth of her lips.

There was nothing else but him and Naomi. He wove his fingers through her thick curls and held her like that, anchored to him, and kissed her. He both gave and demanded, and Naomi matched him want for want. She arched her body against him as if needing to be closer to him, as close as she could get under the circumstances.

He fell backward on the sofa and she gripped his shoulders as if she needed something to hold her to earth. He palmed her bottom as his mouth left hers. He kissed the tender skin along her jaw until he made it to her neck. His tongue traced the line of collarbone until he came to her ear and suckled.

"Lucius." Naomi's moan caused him to remember their location.

"Baby." Lucius held Naomi in his lap as he lifted them from the sofa. "We have to remember where we are." Naomi always made him feel like a randy teenager in the back of a pickup truck.

Naomi blushed. "Yes. You're right."

"Plus, I didn't tell you everything I had to tell you."

Naomi's brow rose. "There's more?"

"Oh, yes," Lucius said. He set her back on the down on the sofa and reached into his suit pocket. Producing an envelope, he handed it to her.

"What's this?"

"Open it." He couldn't wait for her to see what was inside.

Naomi stared at Lucius for several long beats before she finally slid her index finger under the flap to open the envelope. It was an official-looking legal document. She glanced at him, fearful. Was she going to like this?

"Read," he ordered.

"All right, all right." She began scanning the document. As she continued to read, she was stunned by what she read. He didn't! Surely, this had to be some sort of mistake.

Naomi glanced up at Lucius. "I don't understand."

Lucius smiled broadly. "Yes, you do." His smile showed off his perfect white teeth.

"But—but it says that you bought Kelsey's shares and are signing them over to me?"

"That's right, baby," Lucius said. "It's my gift to you."

"But I thought..."

"You thought wrong. Brooks and Johnson is your baby, and you deserve the right as majority shareholder to lead it into the future. I would like to share it with you and maybe give you a few ideas, since I do own 30 percent of the company."

"Oh, Lucius." Naomi's eyes welled with tears at not only his generosity, but his love. Because that's exactly what this was. He was showing her that he loved her and wanted *only her.* "I would love your help. We can run B and J together."

"Are you sure?" This time he sounded unsure. "I don't want to step on your toes."

She nodded. "I'm sure." She was so touched by his generosity and that he would give up his own ambitions for her. "I can't believe you arranged this and that Kelsey agreed."

"Oh, your bestie told me I was signing my death warrant if I didn't live up to my word."

"You've—"

She never got another word out, because Lucius lowered himself to the ground on one knee.

Lucius plucked a ring box from inside his suit pocket and held it in front of her. "Be my wife? And make me the happiest man alive," he said with a large grin.

"Oh, my God!" Naomi's hand flew to her mouth. In her wildest dreams, she'd never imagined this. That Lucius, the love of her life, would not only love her as much as she loved him, but wanted to *marry her*? Surely, she had to be dreaming, so she closed her eyes.

"Oh, no, you don't." Lucius squeezed her hand. "Open your eyes, baby. 'Cause this isn't a dream, and I don't want you to miss a single moment."

Slowly, Naomi opened her eyes, and the love she saw shining in Lucius's eyes was the same she'd seen in her own that very same morning. "Neither do I. It seems like I've been waiting my whole life for you, Lucius."

"So is your answer yes?" Lucius asked. His dark eyes peered into hers. "Because I'm getting kind of anxious down here."

"The answer is a definitive yes." Naomi wound her arms around his neck.

When they pulled apart, Lucius slid the round five-carat halo diamond ring on her finger. "It's beautiful," Naomi gushed, helping him up onto the couch. "It's just beautiful. Just like you."

"Me? I don't think I've ever been called beautiful."

"How about gorgeous and sexy?" He motioned with her hand for her to continue praising him. "And handsome, and incredibly intelligent. And I'm going to be the luckiest woman in the world to have you as my husband."

"No, I'm the lucky one," Lucius said, "because I was smart enough not to let the best thing that ever happened to me get away."

Chapter 20

Later that night, after they'd told Naomi's parents the good news and celebrated with champagne, Lucius returned to his penthouse with Naomi. He didn't care if the press was still stalking him, waiting to see his next move. His statement several days ago had been less than forthcoming, and they were all eager to see what the millionaire playboy would do next. Little did they know that he was hanging his player card up for good.

Even Adam had been shocked when Lucius had shared not only his engagement to Naomi, but that he'd gifted her Kelsey's stock. His best friend had called him insane, but when he'd seen how happy Lucius he was, he'd offered his congratulations. And now Lucius could finally do what he'd been dreaming about all day—take Naomi to bed.

Unfortunately, his cell phone rang, interrupting their moment and allowing his fiancée to slip away into his bedroom.

"Hello?" Lucius asked roughly, since he didn't recognize the number on his caller ID.

"Lucius Knight."

The curt and businesslike tone of the male voice on the

other end caused Lucius to stop uncorking the bottle of champagne he held. "Yes?"

"This is Robert Kellogg, Arthur Knight's attorney. I sent you an invitation to the reading of his will several days ago and never heard from you on whether you intended to attend."

Lucius glanced down at his watch. It was well past 8:00 p.m. "Do you always make a habit of calling your former client's family after business hours?"

"If he was a personal friend, yes," Robert answered. "And since the reading of the will is tomorrow, I'd rather know what's ahead, given how your presence could create a volatile situation with the family."

"My presence?" Lucius snorted. "You mean my existence, Mr. Kellogg?"

He ignored the dig. "So will you be attending? I'd like to prepare Charlotte. As I'm sure you're aware, this has been a trying time for the Knight family."

Lucius thought about Arthur's wife screaming at his mother and how she'd called him a bastard for everyone to hear. "I couldn't care less about the family's feelings."

"That may be the case, but you're now a part of it, Mr. Knight and as such, your presence is required."

Lucius's blood boiled. He didn't want or need this aggravation—not today, not when Naomi had agreed to be his wife.

"So can I consider your attendance confirmed?"

He didn't appreciate the haughty or presumptuous nature of the attorney. "No, it's not. And whether I decide to attend or not, it will be *my decision*, Mr. Kellogg. So I guess you, Charlotte and the entire Knight clan will just have to wait and see."

Click.

Lucius relished hanging up on the snobbish lawyer. How

dare he talk down to him like he had the right to? Lucius Knight was no one's pushover.

"Baby…are you coming to bed?" He heard Naomi's voice softly calling from the direction of his bedroom.

Lucius turned to his bedroom door. He would think about the will and his new family tomorrow. Tonight, he wanted to be with his lady love.

He quickly uncorked the bottle and took it along with two flutes to the bedroom. When he arrived, he was greeted with Naomi leaning against the doorway of the master bath with her robe open. She was wearing a sexy red bustier, garter belt and thigh-high stockings. He darn near lost hold of the champagne bottle in his hand and set it on the dresser nearest him while he stood still, mesmerized by her beauty.

"You look hot!"

"That was what I was going for."

"How long have you had that getup?"

Naomi shrugged as she playfully let the robe slip from her shoulders and strolled toward him. "Oh, I don't know… awhile." She twirled a curl between her fingers.

When she reached him, Lucius growled low in his throat and pulled her to him, kissing her, hard and quick. His body was on fire with a need to have her.

She undressed him, first his shoes and then one piece of clothing at a time. As each item fell in a pool at his feet, desire took over. And when she finally reached his waist, she relieved him of his belt, pants and underwear in one fluid movement until he stood naked and completely aroused.

"Is it my turn?" he asked, stepping away from his clothes, unashamed of his erection jutting forward.

She nodded. "Oh, yes, you can unwrap your gift." She

backed away from him and slid onto the satin comforter on his king-size bed.

Lucius moved forward like a panther, sliding onto the bed and over her.

Naomi's body trembled as Lucius unclasped her bustier and garter belt and slid her barely-there thong down her legs. Once he'd relieved her of her ensemble, he made sure she was ready for him by pushing one finger inside her. She was already wet for him. Would always be. She'd always wanted Lucius. And that would never, ever change.

Lucius fished a condom out the drawer of his nightstand and made quick work of rolling it on and rejoined her on the bed.

She wove her hands around his neck and kissed him deeply as he moved back into position over her, poised to take possession of her body, of her soul. She parted her thighs for him, and he glided inside her with one erotic thrust. Naomi focused on the pleasure that was building inside her, but this time it was different between them. It was deeper, more intense because they had confessed their love for one another.

As Lucius kissed her neck, her collarbone, and lowered his head to take one of her nipples into his mouth while his other hand molded the other breast, Naomi arched to meet his thrusts.

"More, Lucius…" she moaned.

He obliged and his thrusts became faster, harder. Naomi wrapped her arms around his neck holding him to her as her orgasm hit her with full force.

"Lucius!" she shouted.

Lucius's control was slipping. His hands moved to Naomi's hips as he tried to slow down his movements, but Naomi was gyrating her hips and taking him deeper and deeper inside. And when her entire body contracted around his shaft, he was lost.

And when she slid her tongue over his jawline, every vestige of control he'd been trying to maintain, to make it last between them, vanished and Lucius's body began to shake. A loud groan escaped his lips.

Pleasure.

Happiness.

That's what Naomi brought to him. And would always bring. He didn't move; he didn't want to extricate himself from being entwined with her body. He could stay like this forever. And now they always would be. Naomi was his forever.

Much later, after they'd succumbed to sleep, Lucius awoke with Naomi's head lying on his chest. He stroked her damp curls and she glanced up at him.

"Hey, sleepyhead," he whispered, looking down at her.

"Hey, you. You've exhausted me."

"I could say the same," Lucius responded.

A wide grin spread across Naomi's face. "Well, I had to get your mind off the reading of the will tomorrow and onto more important things."

Lucius frowned. "You heard?"

Naomi nodded. "I didn't mean to eavesdrop, but when you raised your voice, I was concerned."

"Well, you don't have to worry. I'll deal with it on my own. I'll go there tomorrow and face my new family, who probably wish I'd go back under the rock I crawled out from under."

Naomi slid up toward Lucius. "But you don't have to, honey. Not anymore. You'll never be alone again, because you have me. I'm coming with you."

"You are?"

"Absolutely. We're a family now. You and me." She pointed to his chest.

"I guess I never thought about it like that—because I—I've never been in love before, Naomi. Never been this happy. Never thought I could be."

"Neither did I, but I am so happy and I can't wait to be your wife and your partner. And it's why I will always be here for you, because you're the one for me, Lucius."

"And you're the woman for me."

Epilogue

The next morning, Lucius wasn't nervous about attending the reading of Arthur Knight's will. Why should he be? He hadn't even known the man. Sure, he'd read the dossier Adam had drawn up, but it told him nothing. He was certain that his presence would cause an uproar among the Knight clan. They were a tight bunch, or so he'd read. None of them interested him much except Maximus Xavier Knight, heir to the throne.

Maximus Knight was Lucius's half brother, a brother Lucius had known nothing of until that fateful night at the hospital when Charlotte Knight let the cat out of the bag about Jocelyn's longstanding affair with her husband. But it was Maximus whom Lucius longed to know. He'd always wanted a brother, someone to talk to and, in this case, since Lucius was older, look after.

But that had never happened, thanks to his mother's machinations. Much, he was sure, to Charlotte's disdain, he was here with his mother, Jocelyn, since she too had been named in the will along with him. But he wasn't alone—his fiancée was by his side.

What would he do without his Naomi?

Lucius certainly wouldn't have come here to this mausoleum the Knights called a house, but he also wouldn't have found the love of his life. How could he have known that hearing about that IPO a year ago would cause him to buy up stock in Brooks and Johnson and lead him to this moment? Lucius certainly wouldn't have thought it.

He'd been content with his bachelorhood until a feisty curly-haired beauty had entered his life. Meeting her was the single best thing to ever happen to him, and it was because of her that he would get through this day, no matter how hard.

"Ahem." A loud cough echoed from the front of the room as Robert Kellogg, Arthur's attorney, stood in front of the small gathering in the library of the Knight family home. "Thank you all for coming and attending the reading of the will for the late Arthur Knight, one of my oldest and dearest friends."

Lucius rolled his eyes upward. When he did, he caught sight of Maximus watching him warily from across the room as he sat with his mother, Charlotte, holding her hand. He sat rigidly upright in his chair in a classic suit that spoke of old money.

"Well, let's get right down to it," Robert said. He pulled out the legal document from his briefcase and began reading. "'I, Arthur Knight…'"

From his side, Naomi squeezed Lucius's hand, and he gave her a sideward glance. She mouthed, *You okay?*

He nodded and lowered his head. He wished Kellogg would just get on with it. Lucius couldn't care less about the old man's bequests to charitable organizations or giving away his most prized jewelry, vehicles and horses. Why was he here? What was the purpose? Arthur Knight had never claimed him in life. Why should he claim him in death?

He soon learned.

"When it comes to the disposition of Knight Shipping, I bestow 49 percent equally to my firstborn son, Lucius Knight, and to my youngest, Maximus Xavier Knight, with 2 percent to my dear girl, Tahlia Armstrong, for always listening to an old man."

"What!" Maximus rose to his full height and glared over at Lucius. "What the hell, Robert? He—" he pointed to Lucius "—gets half of Knight Shipping?" He shook his head. "I won't accept this. I've been groomed to run this company since the day I was born."

"He's right." Lucius rose from his chair, shaking off Naomi's pleas to sit down. "This can't be—you must have gotten it wrong. Why would he leave me stock? I don't know anything about the shipping business."

"It's true," Robert advised. "It was your father's wish that *both* his sons run his empire, Lucius. And you'll learn."

"I can't believe this." Stunned, Lucius sat down with his head between his hands. "Why would he do this? What could it possibly accomplish?"

"It was your father's desire that you two—" Robert looked at both men "—learn to work together, to become brothers one day. He felt like he owed you that after keeping you apart."

"And how are we supposed to do that?" Maximus bellowed.

"One day at a time," a feminine voice said from behind them.

Both Lucius and Maximus turned to stare at the quiet

yet stunningly gorgeous woman standing behind them.
"And who the heck are you?"

"I'm Tahlia Armstrong, your partner."

* * * * *

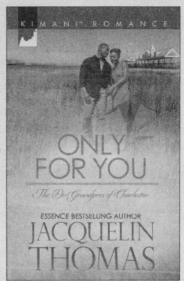

REQUEST YOUR FREE BOOKS!

2 FREE NOVELS
PLUS 2 FREE GIFTS!

KIMANI™
ROMANCE

Love's ultimate destination!

The porch light flickered, casting the area in shadows.
She'd been meaning to change that bulb.

"Thanks again," she said, getting her keys out of her
purse.

Jacobe took her elbow in his hand and turned her to
face him. He stood so close that she had to tilt her head
even farther back to meet his gaze. In the flickering light
of the porch, she couldn't make out the expression in his
eyes.

"I respect your honesty, Danielle." His other hand
came up to brush across her chin. "Don't think this kiss
means otherwise."

Her heart fluttered and anticipation tingled every inch of skin on her body. "Who said you could kiss me?"

His dark eyes met hers and the corners of his mouth tilted up in a sexy smile. "Tell me I can't and I won't."

The air crackled around them. Sparks of heat filled her chest. Her eyes lowered to his lips. Full and soft. Based on the smoldering heat in his eyes, his lips desperately wanted to touch hers.

"One kiss," she whispered.

Don't miss FULL COURT SEDUCTION
by Synithia Williams, available February 2017
wherever Harlequin® Kimani Romance™
books and ebooks are sold.